"I was trying to catch a killer!"

Carley's chin came up.

"How? By getting murdered?" Sloan couldn't believe his ears. "Have you lost your mind?" He heard the raw emotion in his voice and for some stupid reason, he couldn't make himself shut up. "You're not bulletproof and I don't want you taking those chances again. Understand?"

Carley stepped away from him just as Sloan shifted to the other side—and somehow they were practically touching. Suddenly he became very aware of that. She stared at him, as if she was waiting to figure out what he was about to say or do. Sloan started wondering the same thing himself. The eye contact made the air change between them. It created a steamy fog in his brain. Something he definitely didn't need, because he knew he was about to make the biggest mistake of his life. Knowing it, however, didn't stop him.

He lowered his head and touched his mouth to hers....

DELORES FOSSEN

TRACE EVIDENCE IN TARRANT COUNTY

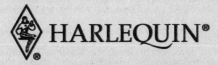

HARLEQUIN®

TORONTO • NEW YORK • LONDON
AMSTERDAM • PARIS • SYDNEY • HAMBURG
STOCKHOLM • ATHENS • TOKYO • MILAN • MADRID
PRAGUE • WARSAW • BUDAPEST • AUCKLAND

To Sgt. Marrie Garcia, Texas Rangers,
for answering all my questions.

ISBN-13: 978-0-373-69238-5
ISBN-10:   0-373-69238-2

TRACE EVIDENCE IN TARRANT COUNTY

www.eHarlequin.com

Printed in U.S.A.

ABOUT THE AUTHOR

Imagine a family tree that includes Texas cowboys, Choctaw and Cherokee Indians, a Louisiana pirate and a Scottish rebel who battled side by side with William Wallace. With ancestors like that, it's easy to understand why Texas author and former air force captain Delores Fossen feels as if she was genetically predisposed to writing romances. Along the way to fulfilling her DNA destiny, Delores married an air force Top Gun who just happens to be of Viking descent. With all those romantic bases covered, she doesn't have to look too far for inspiration.

Books by Delores Fossen

HARLEQUIN INTRIGUE

Don't miss any of our special offers. Write to us at the following address for information on our newest releases.

Harlequin Reader Service
U.S.: 3010 Walden Ave., P.O. Box 1325, Buffalo, NY 14269
Canadian: P.O. Box 609, Fort Erie, Ont. L2A 5X3

CAST OF CHARACTERS

Sergeant Sloan McKinney, Texas Ranger—
He returns to his hometown to investigate two
murders—one cold and one red-hot. The outcome
could tear his family apart.

Sheriff Carley Matheson—A rookie who feels she
has a lot to prove, and solving two murders would be
a start. What she hasn't counted on getting in her way
is her intense attraction to Sloan.

Lieutenant Zane McKinney—Sloan's "golden boy"
brother and the Ranger in charge of the murder
investigation.

Jim McKinney—Sloan and Zane's father. He's a
former Texas Ranger whose career and life were
ruined when he was indicted for murder sixteen years
ago. The charges against him were dropped, but Jim's
name has never been cleared.

Stella McKinney—The long-suffering wife of
Jim McKinney. Beneath that delicate exterior beats
the heart of a woman who'd do whatever it takes to
keep her husband out of jail.

Leland Hendricks—He'll do anything for money,
even fake his own toddler's kidnapping and murder.
But will he go so far as to kill his wife, stepdaughter
and anyone else who gets in his way?

Donna Hendricks—Leland's bitter ex-wife.

Rosa Ramirez—The nanny who adores Leland and
Donna's toddler son. Just how much does she know,
and how long is she willing to stay quiet?

Chapter One

Sgt. Sloan McKinney stopped cold when he heard the sound. A snap. Like someone stepping on a twig.

He eased his SIG SAUER from the holster belted around his waist.

That snap was a sound he shouldn't have heard since the wooded area and the back of the police station were off-limits, sectioned off with yellow tape that warned Do Not Cross. It was a crime scene and the very path that a killer had taken.

Not exactly a comforting thought.

Especially since that snapping sound might be a sign that the killer had returned.

Sloan lifted his head, listening. Waiting. He trusted his training as a Texas Ranger. He trusted his instincts. But a bullet could negate all training and instincts, and he had to be ready to defend himself.

"Drop that gun," he heard someone say. It was a woman. Her voice was raspy and thick, and she was behind him.

Hell.

How had she gotten so close before he'd heard her make that snap? And, better yet, who was she? She was no doubt armed. A person didn't usually make a demand like that unless they had something to back it up.

Since he had no intentions of surrendering his weapon or getting killed, he started with the basics. "I'm Sgt. Sloan McKinney, Texas Ranger. Identify yourself."

There was silence, followed by a loud huff.

Sloan hadn't recognized the person's voice earlier, but he could have sworn he recognized that huff.

"Carley Matheson?"

"*Sheriff* Carley Matheson," she corrected with absolute authority.

Sloan mumbled some profanity. Oh, man. He didn't need this. And he definitely didn't need *her.* He could already hear the argument they were about to have before he even turned around to face her.

It actually took him several moments to *face her* though. First, there was the already brutal morning sun that was spewing light from behind him and on her. Sloan had to squint and then he had to look past her .45-caliber Colt automatic to see her face.

Yep, she was squinting, too, because of the sun. And she was also riled.

And, yep, there would be an argument.

Since the argument was inevitable, Sloan decided to go ahead and start it.

"You're supposed to be in bed, resting," Sloan reminded her.

Less than a week ago, Carley had been shot while in pursuit of a killer and she wouldn't be cleared for duty for at least another forty-eight hours.

"I'm fine," she said as if that explained away everything. Carley lowered her Colt. Not gently, either. Her movements were jerky and stiff, and she shoved her firearm into her leather shoulder holster.

She also winced.

Probably because that rough gun shove had pulled at her bandages and caused some pain. After all, the shooter's bullet had apparently sliced through Carley's right side and nicked a rib. She was lucky to be alive.

The shooter's other victim, Sarah Wallace, hadn't been nearly as fortunate.

In an eerily similar way to how her own mother had been murdered sixteen years earlier, Sarah Wallace had been strangled while staying at the Matheson Inn—just a stone's throw away from where they stood and in the very inn owned by Carley's family. The inn where Carley now lived in a converted attic apartment.

Murder on her own doorstep.

That couldn't have been easy for a peace officer to accept. Especially *this* peace officer.

Unless she'd changed a whole bunch in the past

couple of years—and Sloan doubted that she had, Carley would have taken this crime personally even if she hadn't been shot. Justice was her town, and keeping it safe was her responsibility.

Sloan reholstered his own weapon, and because of that wince, he nearly moved closer to check on her. However, Carley's steely expression had him staying put. It'd be suicide to try to get a look at her wound, especially since it would involve unbuttoning the shirt of her khaki uniform.

Definitely suicide.

So why did he even consider it?

Sloan gave that a little thought and he quickly figured out why. Despite the surly glower, Carley Matheson looked vulnerable.

Yeah.

A man didn't have to dig too deep to find it. The vulnerability was there, stashed beneath that khaki uniform, shiny badge and five-and-a-half-foot-tall lanky body. Her sea-green eyes were sleep-starved. Her normally tanned skin was shades too pale. Her brown-sugar hair was pulled back into a near haphazard ponytail that left stray wisps fluttering around her neck. She looked weary.

No, Carley hadn't fully recovered from her injuries and yet she was apparently on the job.

Part of him admired her for that.

The other part of him wasn't pleased that she was in his way. And she was definitely in his way.

"Why are you out here?" he asked.

For a moment Sloan thought she would fire that exact question right back at him. Instead she pointed to the eaves on the backside of the police station. Specifically to the surveillance camera that was mounted there. Or, rather, what was left of the camera. It had sustained some major damage and was no doubt disabled.

"I had it installed early yesterday morning," Carley explained. She walked toward it, propped her hands on her hips and stared up at it.

Sloan lifted a shoulder. "Why? When I was sheriff, we didn't have a surveillance camera."

That earned him a glaring glance. "When you were sheriff, you also didn't have anyone attempt to break into your office, now did you? Nor did someone try to kill two women right in this area. This is definitely a place that needs some 24-7 surveillance."

He knew about the attempted murders. One was Carley's own shooting that'd taken place in the parking lot of the inn adjacent to where they stood now. The other, the more recent one, involved his soon-to-be sister-in-law, Anna Wallace, and the attempt to kill her in the police station itself. Sloan's brother, Zane, was still beyond riled that he hadn't been able to catch the person who'd tried to murder the woman he loved.

Sloan had been briefed about those near deadly

attempts but not about the camera or the first concern that Carley had addressed.

"Someone tried to break into the police station?" he asked.

"Unfortunately, yes." She slapped at the yellow crime-scene tape that the breeze was batting against her side. "I'm surprised you haven't heard. It's all over town."

"I only arrived an hour ago." But Sloan was a little miffed that he hadn't already been informed about this from his brother, Zane—the Ranger who was heading the investigation into Sarah Wallace's murder. Zane had certainly been thorough in his updates about the murder itself and the subsequent attacks, but he'd apparently left out this little detail. It made Sloan wonder if and how it fit into the grand scheme of things.

"You think this busted camera and the attempted break-in are related to Sarah Wallace's death?" Sloan asked.

Her icy glare melted away. "Maybe. The killer might have thought your brother stored evidence inside. After all, Sarah's sister, Anna, did find those papers, the ones that Sarah had hidden. Zane put them somewhere, and the most logical place would be here at the police station."

Since her inflection made it seem as if she had something to add to that, Sloan stared at her.

Their eyes met.

The morning sun was still haloing around her, and despite the khaki polyester attire, she looked…interesting. She smelled interesting, too. Like fresh coffee, cream and honey. Because he was a male and therefore driven by totally stupid urges that could never be logically explained, he felt that punch of *interest* that he often felt when he was looking at an attractive woman.

And Carley was attractive, no doubt about it.

She was also hands-off.

Because in a bottom-line kind of way, they were enemies. Not just regular enemies, either. Big-time enemies with a feud that'd been going on for sixteen years, since Carley was barely thirteen years old. He'd only been fifteen at the time, but time didn't matter when an issue like this was at stake. Even lust and basic attraction weren't enough to make him forget that this was a woman who would do anything within her power to have his father arrested.

Carley had been the primary witness against his father sixteen years ago. Jim McKinney, a decorated Texas Ranger, had been accused of murdering his lover, Lou Ann Wallace Hendricks. If it hadn't been for Carley's statement that she'd seen his father drunk and disheveled leaving Lou Ann's room at the inn, there probably would have been no arrest. No trial.

No total meltdown of his family.

Sloan's family had been ripped apart because of the questionable eyewitness account of a teenage girl. Carley Matheson.

Remembering that certainly cooled down Sloan, and it got his mind back where it should be—on that damaged surveillance camera and her need to have it installed in the first place. In addition to Carley's theory of a break-in to search for evidence, Sloan had a theory of his own.

"The camera overlooks the wooded area where the killer likely escaped," Sloan explained. "That could be the motive for destroying it."

She turned and stared out into the thick woods. "You mean because there's almost certainly some sort of evidence out there."

"You bet, and maybe the killer wanted to look for it without the camera recording it." And that included evidence regarding Carley's own shooting.

Judging from her slight shift of posture, she considered that, as well.

"So how exactly did you end up in the line of fire of a .38?" Sloan wanted to know. Zane had briefed him, but he wanted to hear what had happened from Carley herself.

Carley eased her hands into her pockets. "I was in my office, working late. I saw something move outside the window. Or, rather, I saw *someone* wearing dark pants and boots run past the window and into the woods. I grabbed my gun and hurried out to see what was going on, to see if I could catch up with the person."

"At this point you didn't know Sarah Wallace had been murdered?" he asked.

She shook her head. "I had no idea. It'd probably only happened minutes before I saw this person. Anyway, I went in pursuit, but by the time I got to the parking lot of the inn, he or she had disappeared into the woods. And then *bam.* Next thing I knew, I was face-first in the dirt and it felt as if someone had set fire to my ribs." She drew in a hard breath. "I really want to catch this SOB."

Oh, man. More vulnerability. She didn't quiver or tremble. There was no deep level of emotion in her voice. But that bullet had robbed Carley of something that Sloan understood all too well.

Peace of mind.

"You'll heal," he told her.

She angled her eyes in his direction. "The voice of experience?"

He nodded. "Eighteen months ago, while chasing down a kidnapper, I took one in the shoulder."

The silence settled uncomfortably around them.

Carley looked away, cleared her throat. "The surveillance disk is in my office. I was just about to review it, but then I heard someone skulking around out here, so I came outside to check things out."

Sloan frowned. "I wasn't skulking."

"Then what were you doing?" She didn't give

him a chance to answer. "Oh, wait. This was a trip down memory lane, wasn't it? You're reliving the good old days when you wore this badge and had the town at your feet?"

That last comment set his teeth on edge. "Sure. I do that all the time. Relive the past. Reminisce about that badge." He made sure the sarcasm dripped from his drawl.

"Then I'll leave you to it," she said with dripping sarcasm, as well. Carley started for the back door but then stopped, turned and faced him. "If you're looking for your brother, Zane's not here."

Oh.

She didn't know.

He figured this was about to get real messy.

"Zane's tied up with the grand jury," she added. "Probably won't be back for days. Maybe even weeks."

Sloan didn't think it was his imagination that Carley seemed smug and pleased about that. She no doubt thought that meant there'd be no Texas Rangers around to interfere with her investigation.

He caught onto her arm to prevent her smug exit. "The mayor and the D.A. don't think you're a hundred percent."

She blinked and took her hands from her pockets. "Excuse me?"

"Neither does Zane. By all rights, you should be in your apartment, recovering."

Carley threw off his grip. "Is this leading somewhere or are you trying to undermine my authority? Because you're no longer sheriff of Justice." She hitched a thumb to her chest. "I am."

Sloan searched for the correct way to say this and decided there wasn't one. The only thing he could do was lay it all there, even though he was dead certain it would cause the argument to escalate.

"It's leading somewhere," Sloan told her. "Since Zane is busy with the grand jury, someone needs to take over the investigation."

That got her hands back on her hips. "That's why I'm here at work, so I can do just that."

"You're on the case, Carley." This was about to get even messier. "But only to assist."

She shook her head, opened her mouth, closed it and shook her head again. Her confusion and denial morphed into anger. "Assist whom?"

Sloan braced himself for the inevitable fallout. "*Me*. I'm in charge of the case now. For the remainder of this investigation, I'm your boss."

Chapter Two

Carley figured it was physically impossible, but she thought her blood might be boiling. She certainly felt something fiery-hot racing through every inch of her body.

"My boss?" she repeated. Not easily. She nearly choked on the words.

Sloan nodded. "Zane is leader of the task force for this murder investigation."

He didn't need to add more to that. Carley quickly got the picture, and it wasn't a picture she liked very much at all. It'd been Zane's call as to whom to put in charge and he'd chosen Sloan.

Not her.

To an outsider, Zane's decision would seem like nepotism or even cronyism, but Carley knew for a fact that Zane and Sloan were brothers in name only. They hadn't been real siblings since their father's arrest sixteen years ago. That arrest had parted them like Moses had the Red Sea, with Zane refusing to get involved in anything but his own sterling career. Sloan, on the other hand, had involved himself to the hilt so he could convince everyone, including his brother, that their father was innocent.

"Zane must really be desperate to ask you for help," she mumbled.

Sloan stood there in his crisp Ranger outfit: a white western-cut shirt, jeans, hip holster, snakeskin boots and his shiny silver-peso badge. He was studying her and probably trying to interpret her reaction. Carley didn't have to interpret her reaction to him. She didn't want him back in Justice and she didn't want him meddling in her investigation.

Why Sloan McKinney of all people?

Their history wasn't pleasant—and it wasn't all limited to her testimony against his father. Seven years ago, he'd beaten her out for the deputy's job. That still stung, even now. Carley had wanted that job more than she'd wanted her next breath. And why? Because it was a stepping stone to the next rung in her career ladder: being the top honcho—sheriff.

Something that Sloan had accomplished in record time by becoming the youngest one in the entire county.

He hadn't changed in the handful of years since Carley had last seen him. The same short and efficiently cut dark brown hair. The same sizzling blue eyes.

Bedroom eyes, the girls had called them.

He still had that athletic physique on that six-foot-three-inch body of muscles and, well, good looks. That was his problem, she decided. Sloan McKinney had always been too sexy for his own good. It had opened doors for him. Plenty of them.

"I know you're upset," he commented. "But Zane thought that folks around here would be more likely to talk to me than him. Or you."

Sloan had probably used that leisurely Texas drawl to soothe her, the way he used to soothe horses on his granddaddy's ranch.

It. Did. Not. Calm. Her.

"Zane and you think folks are more likely to talk to you because you used to be sheriff," she clarified through clenched teeth.

Sloan gave her a yep-that-about-sums-it-up nod. "And there's that whole part about Zane knowing that you weren't medically ready to resume your duties. This is a double murder investigation, Carley. A cold case—and a red-hot one. He needs someone who's a hundred percent and he's not convinced that you are."

She would have argued if at that exact moment the pain hadn't pinched at her side. Mercy. When was her body going to heal? It'd been nearly a week. She couldn't take any more time off. Look what these seven days had done. She was no longer in charge of her own investigation.

Sloan was.

Fate was having a really good belly laugh about that. Sloan, her boss. Her working for him.

Because that was practically an unbearable thought and because her blasted side wouldn't quit pinching, Carley went inside so she could sit down. Of course, she wouldn't be able to do that right away. Sloan had those bedroom-blue eagle eyes nailed to her. He was observing her every move—and that wasn't good, because she wasn't moving so well.

Carley casually strolled inside, plucked the surveillance disk from the machine and tried to be equally casual by continuing to stroll into her office.

"You're in pain," Sloan remarked.

She ignored him and eased into the chair behind her desk. "I suppose Zane has already briefed you about the case that you're now officially in charge of?"

He looked ready to call her on her evasive response, but Sloan finally just lifted his hands, palms up. A gesture of surrender.

Carley hoped there'd be more of those before this conversation was over.

"Zane briefed me, of course," Sloan verified. "But I'd like to hear what you have to say about it."

"No, you wouldn't, but you're trying to placate me because you know I'm mad enough to want to hit you with this surveillance disk."

Carley took out her anger on the disk. With far

more force than required, she shoved it into the player.

"Zane didn't tell me about the surveillance camera being vandalized. Or even that it'd been installed," Sloan explained. "He also didn't tell me that you were back at your office, trying to work." His voice was calm enough, but she could see the little embers simmering in his eyes. They weren't so bedroomy now. "He might have missed something else that I need to know."

It was immature, but she huffed.

Sloan huffed, too. Then he dragged a scarred wooden chair from the corner, deposited it in front of her desk and sat down. "Get past your hatred for me. I'll get past what I feel for you. And for the next few minutes remember that you're the sheriff, I'm your temporary boss and that you're giving me a situation report to bring me up to speed on this investigation."

Carley wanted to hang on to her anger and stew in it a little longer, but, by God, he was right. A situation report to a new officer on the scene was standard procedure, and though she didn't like it, she would not violate procedure because of the likes of Sloan McKinney.

She took a moment to gather her thoughts and so she could come up with the most condensed version of facts. The less face time with Sloan, the better.

"Okay. You win. Here's the situation report. As

you know, sixteen years ago Lou Ann Wallace-Hendricks was murdered. She was strangled with her own designer-brand purse strap. At the time, she was married to one of our present suspects, Leland Hendricks."

And her briefing came to a halt. Because what she had to say next would only stir up even more bad memories.

"I'll finish this part," Sloan volunteered. "We also know that Lou Ann and my father, Jim McKinney, were having an affair. The night Lou Ann was killed, you claim to have seen my father in the general vicinity of her room at the Matheson Inn. That led to his arrest." A muscle tightened in his jaw. "And the case against him was dismissed."

"The charges were dismissed only because there were some inconsistencies with the evidence. Your father's name wasn't cleared, and you know it."

He leaned forward, propping his hands on Carley's cluttered desk. He violated her personal space and then some. In fact, Sloan was so close that she got a whiff of his manly aftershave. It reminded her of the woods, summer afternoons, picnics and sex.

Whoa.

What?

Sex?

Carley was sure she looked stunned over that last thought. Since it was a truly disturbing notion, she shoved it aside and tried to repair the fractures in her own composure.

"What's wrong?" Sloan asked.

"Nothing," she snapped. She forced herself to continue. No more picnic, sex or aftershave thoughts. "I was just thinking how pathetic and dangerous it is that no one was ever convicted of Lou Ann's murder."

"Right." He eyed her with obvious skepticism. "Why don't we fast-forward this briefing to what happened a little less than a week ago."

"Gladly," she mumbled. After a deep breath, Carley went on with the report. "Lou Ann's older daughter, Sarah, came back to town. She called her kid sister, Anna, who's an investigative reporter in Dallas, and Sarah asked Anna to meet her at the Matheson Inn. Sarah said she had information about their mother's killer."

"Who knew that Sarah had come back to Justice?" Sloan asked immediately.

"Everybody."

Carley was unable to contain her frustration about that. Sarah hadn't kept her presence a secret, especially from the killer who obviously wanted to silence her. Not very smart. And because of it, Sarah had ended up dead like her mother. Carley hadn't been able to protect her, and it was because of her that Sarah was dead.

She'd have to learn to live with that.

Somehow.

"Now *you* can finish the update," Carley insisted. "Zane wasn't exactly doing daily situation reports to let me know what was going on."

"Because you were recovering from a gunshot wound."

"And because he thought I was out of the picture. I'm not. So, *boss,* why don't you tell me how you plan to catch a killer who's evaded justice for sixteen years?"

He shrugged. "Simple—I'll continue the investigation that Zane started. If the grand jury says there's enough evidence to arrest anyone, that's what I'll do. If not, then I'll reinterview the witnesses—"

"There weren't any witnesses to Sarah's murder."

"Potential witnesses then," he calmly amended. "And, of course, I'll talk to Donna and Leland Hendricks since, according to the papers Sarah had, they're the primary suspects for both murders."

They were. The information that Sarah had brought with her to Justice pointed the proverbial finger right at Leland Hendricks, the wealthiest man in town, and his equally wealthy ex-wife, Donna.

It was a tangled web that reached all the way back to the first murder.

According to Sarah's collection of papers and notes, sixteen years ago Donna Hendricks was planning to pay Lou Ann big bucks to go to the police with the information and evidence that Leland was plotting to fake his own toddler son's kidnapping and murder so he could collect on the massive insurance policy. Donna hated her ex, Leland, because she'd lost custody of their son to him. So if Lou Ann had threatened to tell all about Donna's bribe, it would no doubt have ended what little visitation rights Donna had left with her little boy. To keep Lou Ann silent, Donna could have killed her and then done the same to Sarah.

Of course, Sarah's allegations implicated Leland Hendricks, as well, because he could have killed Lou Ann when and if she wouldn't go along with his fake kidnapping/murder plan. It didn't help, either, when Zane was able to shatter Leland's alibi for the night of Lou Ann's murder. The wealthy oil baron doctored the surveillance video of his estate that night so that it would appear he was home.

And that brought Carley back to her own surveillance disk.

To the best of her knowledge, hers hadn't been altered or faked, and it was entirely possible she could see who had vandalized city property. She might even discover if it was related to the murders. And the two attempted murders: Anna Wallace's and hers.

She hit the Play button and got up so she could retrieve the rest of her breakfast that she'd left on top of a filing cabinet.

Sloan stood, too, and looked at the honey-filled

donut on the paper plate and her cup of still-warm cinnamon cappuccino. "Hey, where'd you get that?"

Sloan's apparent envy made Carley smile. "Main Street Diner."

He moved closer, staring at it. "They make donuts that look that good?"

"They do now that Donna Hendricks bought the place. She brought in a real honest-to-goodness chef."

He flexed his eyebrows. "Donna is one of the prime suspects in these murders."

"Yessss," Carley enunciated in a way that made him seem mentally deficient. "And your point would be?"

This time he lifted his eyebrow. "Doesn't it seem a little reckless buying donuts from a person who might have murdered two women and then taken a shot at you? How do you know she didn't poison it?"

"I don't," Carley said smugly. "But since I've already had one this morning and I haven't keeled over, I think it's safe for me to eat that one. Besides, the killer has no reason to come after me again because I didn't see his or her face, and everyone in town knows that."

She went back to her seat. Or, rather, that's what she tried to do. Unfortunately Sloan was in her way. Carley didn't let that deter her. She moved past him.

His hip brushed against hers.

She noticed.

Judging from the slight unevenness of his breath, so did he.

Both of them ignored it.

"You're going to eat all of that donut?" he asked.

Was it her imagination or did Carley hear his stomach rumble?

She fought a smile. "What can I say—I'm a cliché. A cop with a donut addiction."

She glanced at the monitor when there was some movement so she could see what the camera had recorded. There was some light coming from her office window, and it gave enough illumination for her to see that it was merely two cats that seemed to have amorous intentions. A moment later they disappeared into the thick woods and out of camera range.

Sloan sat down again, volleying glances between her breakfast and the monitor. "You're not going to offer me any of that donut?"

"Didn't plan on it."

He grinned. Sheez, it was that all-star, billon-dollar grin. "That smile won't work on me," she grumbled.

"What smile?" Oh, butter would not melt in his mouth.

"That one you're flashing right now. I suspect it's coaxed many women into lots of things, including clothing removal. But I'm immune to it. And it won't work on parting me from my donut."

The grin morphed. Just a tad. But instead of evoking sultry thoughts, it had a sad puppy-dog look to it.

"Besides," he drawled. "You should be eating something more nutritious since you're recovering from your injuries. When we're done looking at this disk, we can head to the diner and get you some real breakfast. While we're there, I'll have a donut."

Carley didn't like the sound of that. Her goal was to finish this situation report, review the surveillance disk and then get him the heck out of her office so she could continue her own investigation.

Maybe sharing the donut would speed things up.

Figuring this would cause them to skip the trip to the diner, she ripped the donut in half, plopped his half back on the paper plate and shoved it across the desk toward him.

"Thanks," he mumbled, diving right into it. "See? We do have some common ground. Our shared love of sugary, high fat pastries that have no nutritional value."

"You call that common ground?"

Sloan used that smile again. "Hey, I'll take what I can get."

She could have added something snarky—like, he had already gotten everything he could possibly get—but the sugary donut was making her fingers sticky, so she began to eat it.

"I've arranged to meet with both Donna and Leland this afternoon." Sloan tossed that out there in between bites.

Carley didn't know if that was an invitation for her

to join him or if he was merely continuing with his briefing. She decided to go with the option that suited her. "Let me know when and where, and I'll be there."

"At two this afternoon. Here at the police station." He tipped his head to the filing cabinet. "Just how strong are those pain pills?"

Mercy. She'd forgotten all about those. They'd blended in amid the stacks of files and other clutter. "Not strong enough to keep me off this case," she insisted. "Besides, I haven't even taken any of them." She would have added more, would have probably even started a fresh argument, if there hadn't been more movement on the screen.

"It's motion-activated," Sloan commented, his attention now fully on the monitor. He set the rest of the donut aside.

Carley followed suit. Because what she saw captured her complete attention, as well.

No amorous cats this time. It was a shadowy figure. She turned the monitor, hoping for a better angle. Sloan walked around the desk and stood behind her.

"I can't tell if it's a man or a woman," he mumbled.

"I can't tell if it's even human. It looks a little like a scarecrow in a Halloween costume."

"Definitely human. The person's wearing a mask and a cloak."

She studied the image and had to agree. But the

person didn't have just a cloak and mask. There was something in his or her hand. The light from her office danced off that something. It was a glint of metal.

And on the screen Carley saw the gun rigged with a silencer.

That barely had time to register in her mind when there was the first shot.

And it wasn't aimed at the camera.

The gunman saved the second bullet for that.

Sloan reached over and pressed a button to rewind the disk. He stopped it just as the first shot was in progress. Carley saw then what she hadn't wanted to see.

Mercy.

A chill went through her.

"This person wasn't just gunning for your surveillance camera, Carley," Sloan confirmed. "He or she was gunning for *you*."

Chapter Three

"Are you okay?" Sloan asked when he saw the expression on Carley's face.

What little color she'd had drained from her cheeks. Not without reason. She'd just witnessed a recording of someone attempting to kill her.

"The shots were fired at 1:13 this morning," Carley mumbled, obviously noting the time displayed on the bottom of the monitor.

"You weren't here when it happened?"

"No. I finished up work about a half hour before that, but I'd left on the light. I didn't notice it until after I'd locked up and made my way back to the inn." She looked up at him. "I can see my office window from my attic apartment. I figured it wouldn't hurt to leave the light on all night and I knew I'd be back in the office early."

Sloan played around with that a moment and took it to its logical conclusion. "So, because of the light, someone might have thought you were inside here working at 1:13 this morning."

Carley nodded. "It's not unusual for me to be here at that hour."

He didn't doubt it.

From all accounts, Carley was driven to be the best sheriff ever. That included plenty of seventy-hour work weeks, even though technically the sheriff's office was only supposed to open from eight to five, with all calls before and after hours going through dispatch. He figured with Carley around, dispatch wasn't taking many of the calls, because she made sure she was readily available for the citizens of Justice.

Sloan glanced around the room. "The window's intact, no broken glass. I don't see any point of entry for that first bullet."

He watched the steel and resolution return to Carley's eyes, and she got up at the exact second that he headed for the door.

The race was afoot.

She rushed around her desk and then came to a complete stop. That stopped Sloan, especially when Carley caught onto her side.

"It's nothing," she said, no doubt as a preemptive strike against what he was about to say.

Sloan gave her a flat look. "If it's nothing, then why are you holding your side?"

She immediately lowered her hands.

That was the last straw. Sloan stormed toward

her, and before she could stop him—or slap him into the middle of next week—he went after her shirt buttons.

"What in Sam Hill do you think you're doing?" Carley snarled.

Sloan ignored her, and probably because she was in too much pain, she didn't even attempt to fight him off. He undid the lower buttons at her midsection and had a look at the bandage. No blood. No raw, red areas on the skin. That was a good sign. But the edge of the adhesive tape was caught on one of the tender areas where her stitches had recently been removed. So that might be the cause.

"Hold still," he instructed.

And, much to his surprise, she did.

Sloan slathered his hands with some liquid sanitizer that she had on top of the filing cabinet next to her pain meds. Taking a deep breath, he pulled over the chair and sat down so that he'd be at eye level with the bandage. It also put him at eye level with her stomach. And the bottom edge of her bra.

Purple lace.

Sloan couldn't help it. He looked up at her, and when she followed his gaze, Carley narrowed her eyes to little bitty slits. "I haven't had time to do laundry. It was one of the few wearable things that I had left in my lingerie drawer—and why I'm telling you this, I don't have a clue. Because it certainly isn't any of your business."

To punctuate that, she snapped the upper sides of her top together so there was no visible purple lace.

But Sloan didn't need to see it to remember that it was there. Nope. It was branded in his memory.

"I never took you for the purple-lace type," he commented. Partly because it was true and partly because he wanted her mind on something else when he lifted that tape.

She'd already opened her mouth, probably to return verbal fire, but that tape pull had her sucking in her breath and wincing.

"Sorry," Sloan apologized. "It'll only hurt for a second." He worked quickly, before she changed her mind, and he gave the bandage a slight adjustment. "There. Now it won't pull at the skin that's healing."

She eyed him with skepticism and then tested it by rotating her arm. No wincing. No sucking in her breath. Just a relieved expression. "Thanks."

"You're welcome. But you know, if you were at your apartment resting, that bandage wouldn't have shifted."

"And you wouldn't have gotten a cheap thrill of learning that I own a purple bra." She buttoned her shirt as if she'd declared war on it. "By the way, you tell anyone about my choice of underwear and you're a dead man."

Puzzled, he stared up at her. "Why wouldn't you want anyone to know that?"

She dodged his gaze and stepped back. "I don't

want to draw any attention to the fact that I'm female. I already have enough strikes against me without letting people know that I occasionally wear girlie stuff."

Still puzzled, Sloan shook his head. "Why?"

"Because I'm not male. Because I'm the first woman in Justice to wear this badge. Because I don't have the full support of this town." She aimed her index finger at him. "Because I'm not *you.* And despite the fact you've been gone for years, most people still and always will think of you as the sheriff."

Sloan wanted to deny it, but he knew it was true. Despite the advances in Justice, Carley was probably battling a gender bias. He'd been one of the guys. A good ole boy. Many people in town had no doubt thought that badge was made for him. His for a lifetime.

That acceptance hadn't been extended to Carley.

"Just for the record," he let her know, "you don't have to prove anything to me."

She frowned and then mumbled some profanity. After some posturing and a huff or two, the aimed index finger returned. "Let's get something straight, Sloan McKinney. I want no camaraderie with you. None. And you don't want that with me. Remember, you accused me of lying about your father. I accused you of being blind to the truth. I also accused you of being a jerk and an—"

"I get the point," Sloan interrupted. Man, she made it easy to remember the anger. "So here's the deal. I'll work my butt off to solve this case as quickly as possible so we won't have time to develop any camaraderie. Agreed?"

She agreed with a grunt and headed toward the back exit, where they'd entered earlier. Sloan was right behind her. Neither wasted any time once they were outside. They both started scouring the building for that first bullet.

Thanks to the blazing sunlight striking the brown brick exterior, it didn't take Sloan long to spot it. He went to the window and there it was. A bullet lodged in one of the bricks that framed the window directly outside Carley's office. This was obviously the first shot that the gunman had fired in the wee hours of the morning. The shot meant for Carley.

"I checked the exterior this morning, when I was looking at the surveillance camera," she mumbled. "How could I have missed that?"

He could have stated the obvious—maybe she didn't see it because she was exhausted and wasn't medically ready for duty. But reminding her of that would have only started another argument.

Without touching it, Sloan examined the embedded bullet. A .38 slug. Another inch to the right, and it would have gone through the glass and hit anyone who might be sitting at Carley's desk.

Sloan peered through the window and realized

something else. Her high-back chair would have made it impossible for a gunman to see if she was there or not.

Carley obviously realized that, as well, because he heard the sudden change in her breathing. Sloan didn't address her reaction. No sense touching on uncomfortable issues again. So he scanned the area to figure out what'd happened there.

"Sarah's killer escaped into those woods," he surmised, talking more to himself than her. "It's the same path your shooter took."

Carley made a sound of agreement. "And there's evidence out there—footprints, possibly trace fibers, maybe even the bullet that injured me that night. It was never recovered. So maybe the killer planned to scour the woods to retrieve any incriminating evidence, and the camera got in the way."

"Then why fire that first shot into your office?" Sloan asked.

She shrugged, hesitated, but Sloan already had a theory. Unfortunately he didn't get a chance to voice it, because he heard footsteps.

He instinctively drew his weapon and stepped in front of Carley. To shield her. To protect her. It didn't earn him any brownie points. She pulled out her own gun, huffed, mumbled something and then stepped out from behind him so that they were side by side.

It didn't take long for their visitor to appear

around the corner of the building. It was Leland Hendricks, and since he was a murder suspect, neither Carley nor Sloan lowered their guns.

"There you are, *Sheriff Matheson*," Leland barked. He said her name as if she were some annoying insect that he was about to squash. "What the hell do you mean calling me in again for questioning? I don't have time for this. I have a business to run. And until that grand jury says differently, I'm a free man."

Carley slipped her gun back into her holster and tipped her head to Sloan. "He's in charge. Yell at him."

Sloan gave her an aw-jeez-thanks look before he turned his attention back to a possible killer.

The years had been kind to Leland Hendricks. Of course, money and massive ego probably helped. The graying hair and the wrinkles only added to his air of authority.

"You're in charge?" Leland stared at him.

Sloan nodded. "You have a problem with that?"

"You bet I do." He shook his head. "I won't let you McKinney boys railroad me into taking the blame for these murders. I won't become the scapegoat for your drunk of a father who can't keep his pants zipped."

It took some doing, but Sloan forced himself not to react to that. "You're saying you're innocent?"

"Damn right I am."

"And what about the fake kidnapping of your own son? You're innocent of that, too? Because Sarah, your dead stepdaughter, said differently."

Leland probably didn't want to react, either. But he did. Every muscle in his body seemed to tense. "It doesn't matter what that witch Sarah said. Even if I admitted I'd planned a fake kidnapping, you can't arrest me for that. The statute of limitations is on my side. Besides, I've paid in the worst way a father can. My son disappeared that night. I don't know if he's alive or dead."

"You're certain you don't know that?" Sloan asked.

That did not please Leland. The veins on his neck began to bulge. "I have no idea where he is. If he's alive, I don't know who has him or where he's been for the past sixteen years. That's punishment enough."

Sloan shrugged. "It won't be if I can prove you murdered those women. There is no statute of limitations on murder, and right now I'm making you for these killings."

Leland glared at Carley before he turned that glare on Sloan. "You'll never prove it."

"Never say never, Leland," Sloan countered. "Oh, and if you're not there for that interview this afternoon, I'll have you cuffed and brought in just like anyone who disobeys the law."

There was a staredown, and Sloan wasn't the first

to blink. Leland was. He mumbled, "I'll be there," along with some choice profanity, then stormed away, disappearing around the building.

"Well, wasn't that a special way to start the morning," Carley grumbled.

"*That* started the morning," Sloan said, pointing at the bullet lodged near the window. "I'll dig it out and send it to the crime lab."

"Nearly everybody in town owns at least one .38," she reminded him. "And I'm willing to bet there are a dozen or more that aren't registered, so we don't even know about them. Matching that bullet to a specific firearm will be a needle in a haystack."

A slim chance was still a chance, and the truth was, they had little physical evidence to connect anyone to Sarah's murder. The bullet was a start. But he had other avenues to explore.

One of those avenues was standing beside him.

"Maybe this latest attempt to shoot you isn't about something you saw less than a week ago right after Sarah's murder. Maybe this is about the first murder—Lou Ann's? If so, maybe you saw or heard something sixteen years ago that the killer doesn't want you to recall."

"Then why wait all these years to come after me?" she asked.

"Because, other than the killer, you might be the only person in the entire town who was close enough to witness both murders. Either the killer *thinks* you saw something or you *did* see something and you just don't remember it."

Her posture became defensive again. "I remember *everything* about that night, and the only person that I saw anywhere near Lou Ann's room was your father."

"You could have missed something. A few hours before the body was found, you were sitting in that big, comfortable chair in the lobby at the inn, reading a teen magazine with Johnny Depp on the cover."

Her defensive posture went up a notch. "How did you know that?"

"I looked through the window and saw you."

Carley's eyes widened considerably. "What— you're a Peeping Tom?"

"I'm not. I was looking for my father," Sloan calmly answered.

And he'd looked at Carley, too. In fact, she'd distracted him that night. Why? Because for the first time he'd noticed that she was no longer the gangly girl two grades behind him in school. Among other things, he'd noticed that she had breasts. But it was her mouth that had really caught his attention. The heart shape. The full bottom lip. Her mouth was sultry then. And it was sultry now.

Something Sloan wished he hadn't remembered.

"I saw you that night, too." Her voice was low and whispery, as if this wasn't something she wanted to admit. However, her voice didn't have to be loud to grab his attention.

"Where? When?" Sloan asked.

"I heard something and looked out the window. You were walking on Main Street, headed in the direction of your house." She cleared her throat. "That was about an hour and a half before the murder."

She turned and started inside, but Sloan caught onto her arm. "I get the feeling there's more that you're not telling me."

Carley didn't jump to her defense and she didn't huff at his accusation. "I've told you everything that's pertinent to the murder and to this investigation."

Sloan really didn't care for the way she'd phrased that. "Does that mean there are other *nonpertinent* things you haven't told me?"

She didn't answer. Which in itself was probably an answer—yes, she was withholding something. Carley eased out of his grip and she walked back into the building.

Sloan didn't want to dwell on it. After all, Carley wasn't the type to withhold vital information that would affect the outcome of the case.

So what secrets did she have?

The question settled hard and raw in his stomach. Because it made Sloan search his own memory. It made him recall things about that night. Specifically something that had haunted him for the past sixteen years.

It haunted him now.

Carley Matheson wasn't the only one keeping secrets.

Chapter Four

Does that mean there are other nonpertinent *things you haven't told me?*

Carley frowned.

Sloan's question kept flashing like a neon sign in her head. Either she was missing the gene that could supply her with a poker face or Sloan was psychic. Because there was indeed something "nonpertinent" that she hadn't told him. Nor would she. It was just one of those totally embarrassing events that a woman didn't want to have to recount aloud.

Especially since *Sloan* was that nonpertinent detail.

Yes, she'd seen him that night, but seeing him wasn't all she'd done. She'd stepped out the side door of the inn and watched him, well, walk down the street. She'd even followed him for a few minutes. At the time, she'd blamed the voyeurism on boredom, the sweltering summer heat and her leftover lusting brought on by that magazine picture of Johnny Depp.

But she had to blame it on Sloan, as well.

That night, she'd finally figured out what the other girls had meant about his bedroom eyes. Oh, yes. He'd stirred things in her that even Johnny Depp hadn't managed to stir, and that was something Carley planned on taking to her grave. Sloan was already cocky enough without learning he'd had that kind of effect on her. She wasn't about to be labeled a Sloan McKinney groupie.

"You're awfully quiet," Sloan commented.

Sitting at her desk, she glanced up at him. He was in the doorway, his hands bracketed on either side of the frame, and he was staring at her. Specifically he was staring at her mouth. Probably waiting for her to explain herself.

Uh-oh.

It was time to get this conversation back on something it should be on—the case.

"I'll have one of the deputies start the gun roundup for the .38s," she informed him. "Then the crime lab can do the ballistics tests and compare that bullet lodged in the brick to the guns from the town."

Sloan pushed himself away from the door and stepped toward her. He reached over and ejected the surveillance disk from the computer. "And I'll send this to the crime lab, as well. They might be able to enhance the image so we can figure out who fired those shots."

"Yeah," Carley mumbled, recalling both the image and the shots. "It'll be nice to know who wants me dead."

Their eyes met before he leaned back away from her. "I'm sure it's not personal."

"Somehow that doesn't make it any easier to accept." Carley decided it was a good time to sign the time sheets centered on her desk. It was a necessary task and it would prevent any more eye contact with Sloan. "And you're wrong. It is personal. Very personal. In all probability, someone I've known my entire life is out to murder me."

"Something that neither of us will let happen," Sloan assured her. "Now that we know what we're up against, we can take precautions."

That got her attention off the time sheets. Heck. Eye contact again. "What precautions?"

"Well, for starters, you shouldn't be working late here alone. Not that you'd have time for that anyway. The case should keep us both busy." He motioned in the general direction of the lodged bullet. "In addition to the ballistics and reinterviewing Donna and Leland Hendricks, there are those papers that Sarah brought with her to Justice."

Since that sounded like a prelude to something, Carley sipped her now-cold cappuccino and waited. She didn't have to wait long.

"Carley, if we're going to work together on this

case, it means we're going to *be* together. As in physically together. A lot."

She took the safe approach and tossed out a hopefully confident-sounding, "So?"

"*So,* can you handle that? I mean, it's obvious you can't stand the sight of me."

Well, she apparently had a poker face after all. "I don't have to like you to do my job."

"Does that mean our past isn't going to get in the way?" he asked.

"Oh, it'll probably get in the way," Carley readily admitted. "But above all else, we're lawmen. *Focused* lawmen. Solving this case is as important to you as it to me." She drank more coffee. "And speaking of doing our jobs, you mentioned those papers that Sarah Wallace brought to town. Where are those exactly?"

"I have copies of them."

That was it. *I have copies of them,* and no offer to share them with her.

"And?" she prompted.

"There's a problem with what Sarah had with her when she was murdered." He sat on the corner of her desk. "Basically the papers are a collection of notes and copies of notes that implicate both Leland and Donna."

Carley shrugged. "That doesn't sound like much of a problem to me. If they're guilty, we just arrest them both."

"The notes don't prove murder—even though that's obviously what Sarah believed or she wouldn't have tried to get them to her sister. At worst, the notes and copies are gossip and innuendo. At best, they point fingers at Leland and Donna for some dirty dealings and shady behavior."

That improved her mood. "Anything we can arrest them for?"

Sloan shook his head. "Time's run out to prosecute them on those accounts."

The improved mood didn't last long. "So what's in Sarah's copies that we *can* use?"

"I guess the papers are good for painting a picture of what was going on in the Hendricks household about that time. Lou Ann's copying and hiding habits weren't limited to Leland. There are receipts for prescription painkillers and booze that the nanny, Rosa Ramirez, bought for Donna. God knows where Lou Ann found those."

Carley frowned. "Why would the nanny be buying those things for Donna?"

"My guess? Donna wanted to keep up the appearance of a clean and sober socialite. Her father was still alive back then. You remember how he was."

Yes, she did. And Donna's old-money dad definitely wouldn't have approved of a drugged-out, drunk daughter who might tarnish the family name. "Anything else in Sarah's stash of info?"

"There's a copy of a bank statement that basically proves Leland was broke at the time he planned his son's fake kidnapping and murder."

"That's old news," Carley mumbled.

Sloan made a sound of agreement. "In fact, the reason Leland had come up with such a ridiculous scheme was because he was desperate for money." He paused. "Unlike Donna. She had the cash, but she had it hidden away in trust funds and foreign accounts."

Carley made a mental note of that, but she didn't immediately know how it would help them build a case against either Leland or Donna.

Or even if there was a case to build.

"Is there anything you've seen in those papers and notes that'll help us solve these murders?" she asked.

"I've just scanned through them, but I hope after all the pages are thoroughly examined that Lou Ann and Sarah will be the ones to give us the ammunition to make an arrest. Because Leland's right about one thing—we can't nail him on the fake kidnapping plot. We either get him for murder or he walks."

"And if Leland walks, then maybe that's because he's innocent." Carley didn't wait for him to respond to that. "Of course, I'll want to look at Lou Ann's and Sarah's collection of notes and papers."

Nothing. Nada. Only that drilling stare. It seemed to last for hours before he finally nodded.

Just a nod.

Not exactly an enthusiastic endorsement for her investigative abilities, and so much for his assurance that she would assist him on this case. But it didn't matter. She would study those papers, and this would be her chance to prove to Sloan that she was a good cop.

"I have some reports I have to do for Zane," he let her know. "Then we'll talk about the ground rules for Lou Ann's papers."

Carley was certain that she blinked. "There are ground rules?"

"Yeah. You're guaranteed not to like them, but they're a necessity if we want to keep you safe." Sloan went to the cabinet in the corner and took out a small plastic evidence bag. "For now, I'll dig out that bullet. My advice? Don't try to assist, because all that reaching and moving will only aggravate your injury."

She had no intentions of assisting. She needed a reprieve from Sloan. Judging from the speed with which he made his exit, Sloan needed some time away from her, as well.

Unfortunately her reprieve didn't last long.

Mere seconds.

Before Carley heard the brass bell jingle—an indication that someone had come in through the front entrance of the Justice police station.

She checked her watch. It was a half hour too

early for any of the deputies to arrive for duty, and maybe because she was still jumpy about that bullet being fired at her, she sprang to her feet. The sudden movement tugged at her injury, but Carley tried not to react. She made sure she could draw her gun if it became necessary.

"Sheriff Matheson?" someone called out. "It's me—Jim McKinney."

She didn't relax one bit. In fact, she moved her hand to the butt of her gun. Because, simply put, Jim McKinney could be the person who wanted her dead.

Carley heard the footsteps come closer. Cowboy boots thudding on the hardwood floor. The thudding stopped when Jim McKinney appeared in her doorway.

"It's a little early for a visit." Carley nearly groaned when she heard her own voice. It was actually shaky. She cleared her throat, squared her shoulders and continued. "What can I do for you?"

Carley looked him straight in the eyes. Eyes that were obviously the genetic source for Sloan's own intense baby blues. Jim's, however, were cragged with wrinkles at the corners. It didn't detract from his good looks. Nope. These were character lines.

As if that face needed anything else to give it character.

Jim slipped off his pearl-gray Stetson and held it against his chest. It was almost a submissive kind of pose, but there wasn't anything submissive about his expression. Besides, he wasn't the kind of man who could look totally docile. *Ever.* The well-worn Stetson helped. The tail of a rattler dangled from the silver-rope hatband.

"I came by to talk," Jim explained. "About the murder investigation."

Carley didn't want to be, but she was highly flattered. A suspect was actually treating her like the sheriff. A rare occurrence.

"I hadn't planned to reinterview you anytime soon," she informed him. "Mainly because Zane already did."

Jim nodded. "But I figured you'd have some questions of your own."

"As a matter of fact, I do." Carley just hadn't expected to be asking them so soon. Her hands went on her hips. "Okay, let me just say what's on my mind. Most suspects don't volunteer to be interviewed, and your presence here makes me suspicious. Making yourself readily available doesn't mean you aren't guilty."

Jim appeared to fight back a smile. "You don't beat around the bush."

"It saves time," she explained.

"Yeah, it does. So I'll just put it all out there, too. Anything I do or say will make you more suspicious. It's just the way things are, Sheriff. You're convinced I killed Lou Ann." He shook his head and plowed his hand through his hair. No more smile fighting. His face was somber now. "And I can't remember half of what happened that night. But I do remember where I was nearly a week ago and, just for the record, I wasn't anywhere near Sarah Wallace or the Matheson Inn."

"But you knew she was back in town?"

"Not until after she was dead." He hesitated a moment. "Sarah called me, though."

That revelation surprised her more than Jim's visit. "You didn't mention that when Zane interviewed you."

"Because at the time I didn't know." His breathing was suddenly weary. "I don't think it's a secret that my wife and I argue. A lot. Well, this morning, right after I got home from work, Stella and I had one of our disagreements. It turned a little ugly on her part, and in the heat of anger she blurted out that Sarah had called me that night. Stella thought I might be having another affair."

"Were you?" Carley asked.

"Not on your life."

"But your wife believed you were."

"Stella often believes that," he said as if choosing his words carefully. "And it's because I've given her mountains of reasons to doubt me. Her doubt was misplaced this time, though. I wasn't having an affair with Sarah. In fact, I hadn't seen that girl in sixteen years."

Not sure that she was buying this, Carley shrugged. "Then why did Sarah call you?"

"Probably to ask about my relationship with her mother. To try to make some sense of what'd happened."

Off the top of her head, that was Carley's guess, too. Sarah had apparently come to town to get a lot off her chest. "And what would you have told her about her mother if she'd asked?"

"I would have said that while I've done plenty of kissing, I refrain from the telling part." He met her gaze. "It would have served no purpose for me to rehash the details of that affair. It was just that. *An affair.* It meant little or nothing to both Lou Ann and me."

He was certainly convincing—about that part anyway. Partly because of that Texas charm that seemed to be ingrained in the McKinney males. Still, that didn't make Jim innocent, and Carley couldn't exclude him as a suspect.

"So why didn't Stella tell you sooner that Sarah had called?" Carley continued.

"Like I said, she thought I was having an affair. Or on the verge of starting one. Stella wouldn't have wanted to play messenger for something like that, so she likely decided to nip it in the bud."

Carley tried to piece all of that together. "You told Zane that you were home the night Sarah was killed?"

He nodded. "I was. So was Stella."

There was some hesitation in his voice when he spoke his wife's name. It was the slightest pause that caused Carley to pounce on it. "You know for certain that Stella was home?"

More hesitation. But Jim still nodded. "Her bedroom door was shut, but the light was on. She was probably reading or watching TV."

"You and your wife don't share the same room?"

His face reddened a bit. "Not in a very long time."

Some arrangement. And in this case it wasn't a good arrangement for Jim McKinney since it essentially put his alibi in doubt. "So Stella can't verify that you were home?"

"No. She didn't see me. I guess a sheriff with a suspicious mind could always say that I sneaked out the window, walked clean across town and strangled a young woman that I had absolutely no reason to kill."

Oh, Carley could think of a reason. "You could have killed Sarah because she knew you were her mother's murderer."

Jim bobbed his head and scratched his chin. "True. But I didn't." His gaze went back to hers. "Carley, I know you don't think much of me. Hell, I don't think much of myself, either. But in my way of seeing things, women are the most fascinating creatures on this earth. I'd rather bed one than hurt one. So, if you're going to accuse me of a particular sin or crime, don't make it the murder of a woman."

The sound of the door must have snared Jim's attention, because he turned in that direction. Carley saw the man's grip tighten on his Stetson.

"Sloan," Jim greeted. Some of his cocky ease evaporated. "I didn't know you were back in town."

"Just got in this morning. I'm taking over the murder investigation while Zane's working with the grand jury."

Jim cast an uneasy glance her way. Carley gave him back that same uneasy glance. "Then I guess I'm talking to the wrong lawman. I was giving Sheriff Matheson an account of some information I just learned."

"Sarah apparently phoned your father the night she was murdered," Carley provided. "According to him, your mother took the call, but she didn't tell him about it until this morning."

Sloan didn't seem overly surprised. "Mom was jealous of Sarah."

"Something like that," Jim verified. "Even if I had gotten Sarah's message, I wouldn't have met up with her. Something like that would have gotten back to your mother, and I wouldn't have wanted that."

Sloan peered around the doorway at her. "Well, Sheriff? Do you have any more questions for him?"

"One," Carley readily admitted. "Did you happen to take a shot at me at one o'clock this morning?"

Jim's eyes widened considerably. "I'm not in the habit of shooting at people. Especially women. And

I didn't shoot at you." He paused a heartbeat. "Any idea who did?"

"Nope. But I wouldn't count on it staying that way. The truth has a way of turning up."

"Not necessarily in Justice," Jim mumbled before turning back to his son. "You'll be staying at the house while you're in town?"

"No. Since I'll be working here pretty much night and day, I decided I'd crash at the Matheson Inn. I booked a room there."

Carley was sure her own eyes did some widening. "Since when?"

"Since this morning."

Good grief. No one ever told her anything. Here, Sloan had booked a room with one of her parents' employees, and no one had thought it important to let her know that a Texas Ranger was going to be staying practically right next door to her.

There was another jingle of the brass bell, followed by footsteps. No cowboy boots this time. Those were dainty, almost delicate steps.

Carley couldn't see their visitor, but judging from the looks of pure dread on both Sloan's and Jim's faces, this wouldn't be a good encounter. Carley figured it was probably Donna Hendricks.

But Carley was wrong.

"Jim," she heard the woman say. And Carley knew before she even turned around that it was Sloan's mother, Stella.

Stella spared her son a glance before aiming those unapproving eyes at her husband. "Jim, what in the name of sweet heaven are you doing here?"

Jim lifted his shoulder. "I wanted to tell the sheriff about Sarah calling me."

"Well, you shouldn't have. You shouldn't be here at all. Not without an attorney."

Stella fanned herself as if she were about to faint. It wouldn't be a first. Carley rarely saw the woman and yet she could recall two instances where she'd personally witnessed Stella pass out.

"Are you okay, Mrs. McKinney?" Carley asked.

"No. I'm not." Stella turned to face Carley. "I feel horrible, yet I found it necessary to get out of bed and come here when I realized what Jim might be doing. I won't have you harassing him like this, understand? We've been through enough because of you."

Sloan stepped closer to his mother. "Mom, he came on his own accord."

"Because he knew that Carley would find out about Sarah's call sooner or later and then she'd have him hauled in here so she—"

"Speaking of Sarah…" Sloan interrupted. "What exactly did she say the night she called?"

Stella cast uneasy glances at all three of them. "I can't remember."

"Try, Mom," Sloan insisted.

There was more gaze-dodging. Some fidgeting.

But finally Stella answered. "She said she wanted to meet with my husband. I told her flat out no. I didn't want Jim anywhere around that low-rent woman." She looked at her husband. "We're leaving now. I can't breathe in this place. I need to get home so I can take my headache medicine."

Stella obviously meant business, because she latched on to Jim's arm and marched him out of there.

That made Carley wonder three things. Why the turnaround in Stella's behavior? The woman seemed actually defensive about her husband, and from what Carley had heard from Zane, Stella wasn't always quick to defend Jim about anything. Also, to what lengths would Stella go to protect her husband? Carley didn't have answers to those questions. But then, she didn't have an answer for the last one, either.

And that last question sent her heart dropping to her knees.

How the heck was she supposed to stay under the same roof with Sloan McKinney?

Chapter Five

Sloan glanced at the items on the small table next to his bed. A briefcase jammed with work. A cold cup of really bad coffee. A cell phone on speaker—and on hold. Finally, there was the remainder of a medium sausage-and-mushroom pizza he'd picked up from the diner on his way back to his room.

Those meager items were the story of his life.

"Sad," he mumbled, shaking his head.

He loved being a Texas Ranger, but when the investigation was as frustrating as this one, it made everything seem meager and futile—including pizza, paperwork and coffee.

He needed a break in the case. An arrest would be even better, and in an ideal scenario that would happen ASAP. Every day the killer was out there was another day the citizens of Justice were in danger.

At the thought of that, Sloan stood, strolled to the window and looked out at his hometown, now in the full throes of darkness. The place hadn't changed much in the thirty-one years since he'd been born. Businesses on Main Street had come and gone during his lifetime, but the buildings and landmarks stayed the same.

Sloan looked closer at one of the nearby buildings and he cursed. What he saw did not please him. The light in the sheriff's office was on, and he could just make out Carley sitting there at her desk.

Hell.

All the deputies had already gone home, and hadn't he told her not to be there alone at night? And hadn't she promised him that she wouldn't be? That was what—he checked his watch—a mere five hours ago. Right after grueling and unproductive interviews with Donna and Leland Hendricks. And right before he'd left Carley to arrange for the bullet they'd taken from the building to be sent to the crime lab. So much for her promise that she was going straight to her apartment to get some rest.

Yeah, right. That didn't look like rest to him. She was definitely working. And she was working alone. Sloan was ready to grab his phone and call her to remind her of her promise, but before he had a chance to do that, he heard his brother's familiar voice.

"Sorry to keep you on hold," Zane greeted. "Things are a little crazy right now."

Sloan knew how he felt. While keeping an eye on Carley, he forced himself to deal with the case.

"Does that craziness involve a grand jury decision so I can arrest either Donna or Leland?"

"Afraid not. There's a lot of evidence and testimony. This could go on for days. Don't guess you've had any luck finding evidence against either of them?"

"Not so far." He glanced at the papers and notes that Sarah Wallace had brought with her to Justice right before she was murdered. Sloan had already skimmed them, but he'd have to start a detailed read of those tonight, right after he got Carley safely back to her apartment. "But maybe soon."

Sloan watched as Carley stood and got something from the filing cabinet. Oh, man. She was right in front of the window, and the blinds were pulled up all the way. She might as well have had a blasted bull's-eye painted on her back.

"How are things at home?" Zane asked.

"Haven't been there yet." Instant guilt. But after their earlier meeting, Sloan decided that guilt was better than the alternative. He wouldn't be able to survive in the same house with his mother. "I'm staying at the Matheson Inn."

"I understand. Fewer distractions than there'd be at home."

"You'd think," Sloan mumbled, still watching Carley. "But I did see Mom and Dad this morning. They came by the sheriff's office. Dad volunteered to be interviewed about Sarah Wallace's murder, and before he could say much of anything, Mom unvolunteered him."

Zane made a *hmm* sound. "Did she say why?"

"Something about not trusting Carley."

"That's not a surprise. Mom *doesn't* trust her."

What Zane didn't mention was that Sloan and he weren't on the same side of this particular subject. Well, at least they hadn't been before this latest murder.

"Dad also told us that Sarah called him the night she was killed," Sloan continued. "And, for the record, he didn't withhold this from us. Dad wasn't home when Sarah called. Mom answered the phone and she didn't tell him about it until this morning when they got into an argument."

Zane paused. "Did Sarah happen to say anything to Mom that we can use in the investigation?"

"Nothing. Dad thinks that Sarah just wanted to talk to him and try to make sense of what happened to her mother."

"You might want to make a point to see Mom and Dad again," Zane suggested.

Sloan didn't like the sound of that and he didn't bother to suppress a groan. "Why?"

Zane's deep breath let Sloan know that he wasn't going to like what was coming. "I've requested that Cole come down to assist you."

Cole. Their half brother.

His father's "love child."

Man, Sloan hated that expression, because Cole's birth certainly hadn't created much love in the McKinney family. Even though Cole was now a grown man—and a Texas Ranger at that—he was also a proverbial thorn in the family's side.

A walking, talking reminder of his father's indiscretions.

"Let Mom know that Cole is coming," Zane continued. "Try to brace her for it."

"Nothing will brace her for that." Carley moved again, snaring Sloan's attention. With a file folder in her hand, she sank back down in the chair behind her desk. "Wasn't there anyone other than Cole who you could bring in?"

"Not really. He's a tracker—the best, from what I've been told—and I need someone to go through the woods to look for evidence."

That evidence included the bullet that'd taken a chunk out of Carley's ribs. Yes, it was important to find that. Because that bullet might also lead them to the killer.

"You got my e-mail about the shot someone fired into the sheriff's office at one o'clock this morning?" Sloan asked.

"I did. Suffice it to say it was a surprise. You think it's related to Sarah Wallace's murder?"

"I don't know. Carley thinks maybe the culprit thought you'd stored evidence in the sheriff's office and that he or she was after it."

"Carley?" Zane repeated.

"Yeah, *Carley.* Why do you ask?"

"I don't think I've ever heard you say her name without adding some profanity. By the way, I apologize for putting you into a situation with her. I know you can't stand the sight of each other—"

"We're working out our differences. Carley's a professional, Zane. She's not going to let bad blood get in the way of finding the killer."

Zane's silence lasted several long moments. "Just how closely are you working with her?"

Sloan's silence lasted a bit, as well. "Not as closely as you seem to think."

"Don't get your boxer shorts in a twist. Remember, I fell in love with Anna and became an engaged man while working on this case. It sounds a little clichéd, but there's something about murder to make a man remember just how precious and short life can be."

That was all well and good, but Sloan didn't want Zane thinking that he wasn't giving this case everything he could possibly give it. "I'm not sleeping with Carley, if that's what you're implying."

"I didn't think you were sleeping with her. You haven't been back in town long enough. Even you don't work that fast, little brother."

"Ha-ha." But even the fake laugh felt good. It'd been too long since he'd had a brotherly conversation with Zane. It was too sappy to admit to his brother that he'd missed him, but Sloan figured Zane had already guessed it.

Heck, maybe Zane had missed him, too.

"I'll give you a heads-up before Cole arrives," Zane continued.

"Thanks." Sloan hesitated before he dived right into what he needed to say next. "One more thing— a surveillance camera recorded the two shots that were fired last night. I sent the disk and the bullet I retrieved to the lab. I wondered if you'd be willing to use your rank and connections to rush it through?"

Zane hesitated. "You're asking me for a favor?"

"Yeah. Don't sound so surprised."

"I'm surprised because you've never asked."

And he wouldn't have this time if it hadn't involved Carley. Sloan kept that to himself.

"I'll check on the disk and the bullet," Zane promised. "You keep things under control there. Do everything you can to find me some evidence I can use."

Sloan assured him that he would and he hung up with the intention of calling Carley so he could chew her out. However, something caught his eye. Some movement deep within the woods behind the sheriff's office.

A shadow.

But a shadow of what?

He moved closer to the window, trying to pick through the darkness so he could decide if it was some bird or another animal that'd ruffled a tree branch. Unfortunately he couldn't tell.

And he couldn't take a chance.

If the shooter had returned, it wouldn't take much to succeed in gunning down Carley.

Sloan grabbed his phone, shoved it into his pocket and strapped on his holster while practically racing out the door. He didn't even bother locking it.

Because he knew the back entrance of the inn would be a semishortcut, he headed in that direction. Once outside, he picked up speed. He probably hadn't sprinted like this since his cross-country days at Justice High.

Sloan skirted the edge of the woods, slapping aside low-hanging branches and hurdling over a pair of fire-ant beds. Thankfully there was a hunter's moon to help him see, so he was able to keep watch of his surroundings to make sure he wasn't about to be ambushed.

The night hadn't cooled the air much, and he quickly worked up a sweat. He also worked up a hefty amount of concern. For Carley. He prayed that she was all right. One way or another, he would get to her in time and stop that shadowy figure from finishing what he or she had started almost a week ago.

Sloan turned, intending to race toward the back door of the sheriff's office, but turning was as far as he got.

Something slammed into him. Hard.

But Sloan soon realized it wasn't *something*. It was *someone*.

And that someone was Carley.

Suddenly his arms were filled with her, and he held on to keep them both from falling. It didn't help. The impact sent them off balance just enough and, despite his efforts, they smacked into the side of the building.

He immediately thought of her injuries and he tried to take the brunt of the impact. Sloan was reasonably sure he succeeded, because he hit the rough brick exterior hard enough to see stars.

Big ones.

"Are you hurt?" he immediately demanded.

"Sloan?" she questioned in between loud gusts of breath. "Mercy, you scared the daylights out of me."

"Well, this didn't do much to steady my heart either. Are you hurt?" he repeated.

She paused a moment as if taking inventory and shook her head. "I think I'm okay." Carley looked up at him, and the moonlight was very generous. He had no trouble seeing her face and the puzzled expression on it. "What are you doing out here this time of night?"

"I was watching you from the window in my room," Sloan heard himself say and actually winced. He couldn't have sounded any creepier if he'd tried.

Judging from the way Carley's mouth dropped open, she felt the same way. "You were *what?*"

"I was on the phone with Zane and I just happened to look out the window and I saw you. And I thought I saw something else."

Because Sloan still had hold of her, he felt her muscles tighten to knots. The puzzlement and surprise were replaced by concern and maybe even fear. "What did you see?"

"A shadow or something."

She relaxed as quickly as she'd tensed. "Yes. I saw that, too. It was the cats again." Carley pushed them away from the building and would have pushed herself from him if Sloan hadn't held on.

"You noticed the cats," he clarified. It didn't take him long to guess why that was, and that realization caused the adrenaline and the anger to surge through him. "You were setting a trap, using yourself as bait."

Her chin came up. "I was trying to catch a killer."

"How? By getting murdered?"

"No. Of course not. I had the surveillance camera repaired this afternoon and I was watching everything on the monitor. If anyone had stepped out of those woods—"

"Hell's bells! Cameras and monitors don't stop bullets," he practically shouted.

"But a Kevlar vest will." Carley patted her chest to indicate she was wearing such a protective garment beneath her shirt.

Sloan patted her forehead. "But it won't stop a

bullet aimed here. Sheez, Carley. Have you lost your mind? You could have been killed."

He heard the raw emotion in his voice, and for some stupid reason he couldn't stop it. Sloan also couldn't make himself shut up. He continued his rant.

"You're not frickin' bulletproof," he snarled. "And I don't want you taking those kinds of idiotic chances again, understand?"

Probably because she didn't like his order—and it *was* an order—she stepped to the side. Away from him. At least it would have been away from him if Sloan hadn't stepped to the side at the same time. Somehow it put them even closer, though they were already touching practically from head to toe. Heck, he still had his arms around her.

And he suddenly became very aware of that.

Well, his body became aware of it first. His mind didn't take too long to catch up. Not good. No part of him was thinking clearly when it came to Carley. For some reason, she had his hormonal number.

Wasn't this been exactly what he'd been fantasizing about all afternoon? Carley and her hot mouth?

She stared at him as if she were waiting to figure out what he was about to say or do. Sloan was wondering the same thing himself.

The eye contact made the air change between them. It was hotter. A lot hotter. It created a steamy fog in his brain. Something he definitely didn't need.

Because he knew he was about to make the biggest mistake of his life.

Knowing it, however, didn't stop him.

He lowered his head and touched his mouth to hers.

Chapter Six

Carley melted.

There was no other word for it. Her entire body seemed to turn to warm liquid. And that intense reaction was just from the briefest touch of Sloan's mouth. Which made her wonder—what would a real kiss do to her?

She fought her way through the melting, mind-numbing effect and she soon realized that this should not be happening. No way.

"We can't," she managed to say. She untangled herself from his arms and she stepped back. Way back. Putting as much space between them as she could manage.

"You're right," he mumbled. And then he cursed. "I should just find a rock and hit myself in the head with it."

All right. It was time to defuse this. It'd already gone miles too far. "Why would you want to hit yourself? That wasn't even a kiss."

He stared at her. "Then what was it?"

"An accident."

"An accident," he repeated. Sloan repeated it again under his breath. "What—our mouths just sort of bumped into each other?"

"Yes."

More staring. Sloan added an eye roll. "Good grief, you're stubborn."

"And you're not?" She returned that eye roll and jabbed her index finger against his chest. "Look, I'm doing us both a favor here, because kissing is definitely a no-no. It's like my purple bra. I don't want the people here to think of me that way and I'm sure you feel the same."

No more eye rolls, but the staring continued and intensified. "Say what?"

"You know exactly what I mean."

"Unfortunately I think I do." He snagged her by the shoulders, forcing eye contact. "Carley, maybe this is a good time to remind you that you have nothing to prove to me or to this town. The city council hired you because you were qualified."

Oh. He'd opened *this* can of worms.

"They hired me because there wasn't anyone else who wanted the job. Lousy pay, long hours and an outdated office and equipment. Not exactly an enticement to most lawmen. In fact, it was so bad that they called me while I was working at the Department of Public Safety and asked if I'd be willing to come back to town to help them out *temporarily*." She took a deep breath. "There. I've said it. I got the job because I had absolutely no competition. And even then it wasn't a unanimous appointment by city council."

"Only because you're a woman." He took a deep breath, mimicking hers. "There, I've said it."

Carley felt that melting feeling again and realized it was as dangerous as a killer's bullet. It could distract them at a time when they needed to be fully focused.

She stepped away again but made the mistake of raking her side against the bricks. Normally that wouldn't have hurt, but the movement tugged at her bandages. The adhesive had obviously shifted again, and it was actually hurting.

Carley tried her best to keep any and all reactions from Sloan. But she failed.

"You're in pain," he informed her.

"A little." She decided it was a good time to head to her apartment. "It'll pass."

Sloan fell in step right alongside her. But that wasn't all he did. He positioned himself so that he was closer to the woods. In other words, he was placing himself between her and a potential gunman.

"You don't have to do this," she complained.

"But I do. I'm the boss, remember? If you were in charge, you'd be walking where I am."

"Right." Though it would no doubt take a massive

argument for that to happen. Sloan was pigheaded and cocky, but he was also a protective male. Carley hadn't thought she would ever feel this way, but for once she was glad he was.

"You didn't argue about our positions," Sloan quickly pointed out.

"No. I've decided I'll use all the help I can get."

A slight sound had her stopping. She stood there frozen until she spotted the owl perched on a live oak limb.

"Are you okay?" he asked.

Because her adrenaline was through the roof, Carley didn't even attempt to lie. "I'm scared. And I know I shouldn't be admitting that to you, but I can't help myself."

"Why shouldn't you admit it to me?" But he didn't wait for her to answer. "Oh, it's another of those purple-bra analogies, huh? People won't respect you if they know you're afraid of real honest-to-goodness danger. Except there's no basis for an argument this time. You have a right to be scared."

"No, I don't. I'm a sheriff and I'm trained to catch bad guys—"

"Someone tried to kill you, less than a week ago and then again just last night. Cops are human, Carley, and getting past something like that takes time and long talks with friends who'll understand."

"Is that what we are—friends?" Carley made certain that she sounded skeptical.

"Well, not really. But we're comrades in the same proverbial boat." They reached the back of the inn, and he opened the door. Or, rather, he tried to and realized it was locked. She extracted her keys, opened it herself, and Sloan practically pushed her inside. "I've got two shoulders, and both of them are yours anytime you need them."

It was a very tempting offer. An offer Carley had no intention of accepting. "I want to feel safe again. I just want this to be over."

"I know. And it will be. Soon."

She started up the stairs toward her apartment. Again, he followed. Again she didn't stop him. That caused her to silently curse. She had to put an end to this. She could *not* continue to rely on Sloan McKinney and his rather ample shoulders.

"How did you get past being shot?" she asked, glancing behind her at him.

"I did what you're doing. I threw myself into the job. I focused on the things I could control."

"Now that's a laugh. I'm not sure I can control anything." She stopped outside her door but didn't open it. "There's a killer out there, Sloan. Someone we both know. Someone who knows me bone-deep. Someone who knows how to come after me. And why? Because I may have seen something the night Sarah was killed. Trust me, other than dark pants and boots, I didn't. I've gone over every detail a million times and I honestly don't know who tried to kill me."

He looked as if he were having some kind of argument with himself. Probably was. Because he sighed heavily and reached for her.

Carley tried to dodge that reach, but he slid his arm around her and eased her closer. Not so they were touching, though. And Carley definitely didn't put her head on his shoulder.

Still…

"This isn't right," she whispered.

"It's innocent."

"It's intimate. Full-blown sex would be less intimate than this."

Sloan chuckled. "Obviously you've never had great full-blown sex."

Carley couldn't help it. She laughed, too. Unfortunately it made her side hurt. "If that was an invitation, I'm not accepting."

"Good. Because you're no in shape for sex, great or otherwise. Want me to check that bandage for you?"

"No, thanks. One look at my purple bra is all you're going to get."

She waited for the humor, maybe another laugh. But it didn't happen. There was no humor in his eyes. Only deep concern.

"You can't play sitting duck again, understand?" he asked. "We're a team, and whatever we do with this case we do it *together.* It's the only way I can make sure I keep you safe."

That brought her chin up a little. It was a knee-jerk reaction. "I could counter that with it's not your job to keep me safe."

"But it is." Sloan shook his head and mumbled something about finding another rock to hit himself in the head. "It's what I'd do for anyone who works for me."

Okay. So it wasn't personal. Thank goodness.

Why didn't that make her feel better?

"Get some rest," he insisted, testing her doorknob. He frowned when he realized it wasn't locked. "Tomorrow morning, we start examining Lou Ann's papers and notes. We'll need to go through each page with a fine-tooth comb."

Her mood brightened immediately. "I'm finally going to get to see them?"

"You'll not only see them, you'll be sick of them before this is over."

"I doubt it. It could break this case wide-open." Carley gave that some thought. "We'll go over them *together* so we can make sure you don't misinterpret anything."

Sloan looked genuinely insulted. "You don't trust me."

"You have a massive blind spot when it comes to your father."

"And you appear to have a fixation with pinning these murders on him. My father is not our primary suspect. Leland and Donna Hendricks are."

"They're two of many."

The corner of his mouth lifted. "We're arguing again. That's a good thing."

"Yes." She smiled. "It feels more natural than the accidental kiss, doesn't it?"

He didn't answer.

Instead Sloan tipped his head toward her apartment. "Check that bandage, eat and rest. Oh—and, Carley, lock your door tonight."

She experienced another of those knee-jerk reactions. "I'm not in the habit of doing that."

"Then get in the habit."

"And what happens when the housekeeper starts blabbing to everyone in town that I lock my door?" She stepped inside, turned and faced him. "That's not a sterling endorsement for the town sheriff."

"Let the housekeeper blab. Let the town think what they will. Just lock your door."

Because that sounded like an order and because Sloan strolled away as if he knew that his order would automatically be obeyed, Carley decided to defy him. She slammed the door between them.

And she didn't lock it.

Why?

Because this killer was a coward, that's why. The shot to the window of her office had proved that. The SOB had tried to shoot her in the back.

That riled her to the core.

But it also meant the killer likely wouldn't show up at her apartment for a face-to-face confrontation.

And that in itself told her something critical about the person she was trying to catch.

Who was the sneaky, cowardly sort who would do just about anything?

Definitely Leland Hendricks.

Donna seemed a little too prim and proper to be skulking around in the woods in her pricey shoes and designer clothes. But then, Carley couldn't see Jim McKinney aiming at a woman's back.

Sarah's and Lou Ann's murders had been crimes filled with passion. Two victims strangled in the heat of the moment. The attempts on her life, however, had been with a gun rigged with a silencer. It was a weapon meant to conceal a crime, which meant pre-meditation. The weapon was also meant to put distance between the killer and the victim. Unlike strangulation, which was "hands-on," the most personal way to murder someone.

So, did that mean there were two people—a killer and a would-be killer who was after her?

While Carley considered that, she unbuttoned her uniform shirt and Kevlar vest so she could check the bandage. It had indeed come loose and was pulling at her skin. It was time for a complete redressing. Carley headed to the bathroom, but she paused a moment to look out the window.

It occurred to her that this was the same view that Sloan had since he was in the room directly beneath her. Heck, he was probably looking out, as well.

Searching those woods for a killer.

Carley searched the woods, too, but her attention came back to Main Street. Specifically to a dark four-door car parked a half block from the inn. She didn't recognize the vehicle, and the windows were tinted. There was also mud or something covering the front license plate.

She mentally shrugged, ready to dismiss it. After all, there was no law against tinted windows, muddy plates and parking on Main Street. But the car pulled from the curb and slowly began to drive away.

With its lights off.

She slid her hand over her stomach to steady it. Normally a slow-moving car wouldn't have elicited such a stomach-tightening reaction. But that was before someone had tried to kill her. Twice.

She considered going after the vehicle, but it'd be long gone before she could even make it outside. Besides, it was probably nothing.

Probably.

But it was that small, niggling doubt and Sloan's order echoing in her head that got her moving back to her door. Because, despite her earlier theory about the shooter being a coward, there was no certainty that he or she wouldn't come after her again.

In her own apartment.

Sloan was right about one thing—no amount of Kevlar could protect her from a direct shot. And nothing was a hundred percent—not even Sloan's assurances that he would stop this maniac from coming after her. If she hoped to do the job she'd sworn to do, she couldn't stay in hiding. She had to get out there.

In the open.

Where her next step could be her last.

And she had to do that while convincing the people of the town that she was as fearless and as brave as the men before her who'd worn the badge.

Carley locked the door, leaned against it and tried to blink back the tears that she knew she couldn't stop.

Chapter Seven

Sloan gulped down the remainder of his second cup of coffee and then motioned for the waitress to pour him another one. Carley quickly finished up her own cup so it could be refilled, as well.

It was her fourth.

And Sloan was definitely keeping count.

Carley mumbled a thanks to the waitress, but she didn't take her eyes off what was in front of her. And what was in front of her were copies of Lou Ann's papers that Sarah had brought with her to Justice. Sloan had given copies to Carley at the start of what was supposed to be a working breakfast. So far, she had done a lot of work in the form of reading the papers and she'd had enough coffee to float a ship, but she hadn't taken a bite of her buckwheat pancakes topped with fresh blueberries.

"Rough night?" Sloan asked once the waitress had stepped away.

She shrugged. "Why do you ask?"

"For one thing, because of the volume of coffee you've consumed. You've also yawned three times, and your eyes are red."

"Must be allergies," she mumbled with her attention still focused on the papers.

Sloan didn't buy that for a minute. "Or maybe, like me, you didn't sleep well. It's my guess you spent most of the night looking out your window, watching for a killer."

"I looked a few times," she admitted. "I take it you did some window watching, too?"

"A little."

Carley hesitated, scraping her thumbnail over the coffee cup handle. What she didn't do was look at him. "Did you see the car?"

Sloan blinked, certainly not expecting that question. "What car?"

"The one parked on Main Street about a half block from the inn. Dark blue, maybe black. Four-door. An obscured front license plate. It drove away with its headlights off."

Sloan no longer needed caffeine. That got him wide-awake. "And after you saw this suspicious car, you didn't think to come and get me?"

That earned him a huff. "I can't come and get you every time something unnerves me."

"Why not?" And he was serious, too. Heck, he wanted her to do just that.

"Because lately everything unnerves me, okay?"

She quickly looked away and stared down at the papers. But Sloan didn't think for minute that she was actually reading them. No, there was something else going on here.

Something that he understood.

Unfortunately it wasn't something he could talk Carley through. Heck, he couldn't even help her. Probably the only thing that would help was to catch the killer so she'd finally feel safe again.

"Maybe we could ask around," he suggested. Best to get her focused on the aspects of the case they could control. "Maybe someone saw the car."

"It was late, well past business hours, and the car had heavily tinted windows. On top of that, it doesn't belong to one of our suspects."

"You don't know that for sure. Leland has at least a dozen employees. He could have borrowed one of their vehicles. The same holds true for Donna." He glanced around the diner. "There are two cooks and three waitresses working right now. Maybe Donna used one of their cars."

"But why would either of them do that?" Carley immediately demanded. "There's no motive for lurking around outside the inn."

Oh, yes, there was.

Sloan could think of a really bad motive.

Maybe the person hoped that Carley would come outside so he or she could take another shot at her. Perhaps Sloan and she had thwarted the gunperson's plan by coming in through the back entrance of the inn.

Judging from the sudden death grip that Carley had on her coffee cup, she suspected that, as well. It could have turned into a fatal walk if they'd chosen to go the route of Main Street.

Sloan saw it then. That slight tremble of her bottom lip. He might have done something to try to comfort her, but she spoke before he could.

"So what's your initial impression of Lou Ann's papers?" she asked.

Sloan considered telling her not to change the subject, but even he had to admit it was a subject that needed changing. Camaraderie was one thing, but there was no reason it had to lead to compassion.

Carley lifted her eyebrow, obviously waiting for him to answer.

"I think Lou Ann was a very calculating woman who wanted to make sure she covered as many bases as possible," Sloan concluded.

"Amen." Was that relief in her voice? Sloan wondered if it was caused by the change of subject or Carley's genuine interest in the notes. Probably a little of both.

"Lou Ann managed to copy a lot of incriminating things when she was married to Leland," Carley continued. "There are receipts for bottles of scotch and drugs for Donna. If Donna consumed half of what was purchased for her, she must have stayed drunk most of the time."

"And probably did," Sloan provided. "She wouldn't have wanted anyone, including Leland, to know that she was drinking that much. He could have—and did—use her alcoholism as leverage to get custody of their son."

"And yet Lou Ann managed to get proof of Donna's drinking. Well, at least proof that the booze and the prescription drugs had been purchased. Lou Ann even got her hands on some of Leland's hand-written memos where he bribed a county official to get a permit to drill oil on a wildlife preserve." She paused. "Do you think Lou Ann planned to black-mail Leland and Donna with all of this?"

"I'm sure that crossed her mind. But, of course, as far as we know, Lou Ann never got around to doing that because she was killed."

"Perhaps by one of the very people she intended to blackmail." Carley made a sound to indicate she was thinking about that. "So here's what I gather from all of the notes and copied memos. Leland was virtu-ally broke. He wanted money and he wanted it fast. So he came up with the fake kidnapping and murder plot so he could collect his son's life insurance policy."

Sloan nodded. "To carry through with the fake kidnapping, Leland wanted Lou Ann to take his toddler son and go into hiding. But Lou Ann wasn't so keen on the idea of babysitting Leland's kid."

Carley picked up on the summary when he stopped. "So Lou Ann contacted an old friend from Vegas who was supposed to come and get the boy."

"In the meantime, Leland was going to fake the kidnapping and make it look as if his son was murdered. He planned to do that by stockpiling some of his son's blood and having Lou Ann plant it at the supposed crime scene. But it all backfired when Lou Ann was killed and...whatever happened to the child?" Sloan asked.

Carley glanced back through the notes. "There's no memo for that. Maybe because Lou Ann didn't know. But there's certainly a lot of detail here, and that makes me inclined to believe that Sarah might have been able to figure out what happened to her mother."

"Me, too," Sloan answered. "In fact, if she'd lived, I think Sarah would have been able to tell us who murdered her mother."

She made a sound of agreement. "And that's the reason I believe Sarah died." Carley tapped the top page. "So do you think the killer saw these papers and realized they could point the finger at him or her?"

"It's possible. Or maybe the person didn't actually see the papers. Maybe Sarah told them. She wasn't exactly tight-lipped about her return to town. Plus, she chose to meet her sister in the very room where their mother had been murdered. Someone would have definitely gotten wind of that."

Carley blew out a deep breath. "We're back to trying to figure out who Sarah called. And how."

"Zane figures that Sarah used one of those prepaid cell phones and that's why we haven't been able to trace any of the calls she made. If we follow through with that, then the killer likely took the phone, because it would have contained his or her number. That would have been a direct tie to a murdered woman."

She nodded, paused. "Well, we know Sarah phoned her sister, Anna, and she called Leland and several former members of his household staff who'd worked for him during the fake-kidnapping escapade. She even called your father."

"Yes. With the exception of the call to our father, Zane verified those calls when he processed the case and took statements from all interested parties. And as for Donna, she could have easily learned that Lou Ann's daughter was back in town and could have made plans to eliminate Sarah before the woman could talk."

He didn't want to think that the same could apply to his father.

Carley groaned. "There's Kimberly Parsons," she mumbled. "She's staring at us."

Kimberly Parsons. His date for the senior prom. He started to look back, but Carley gave him a rather hard nudge with her shoe on his shin.

"Don't look at her," Carley warned. "I don't want her coming over here."

But it was too late. Sloan had already started his glance back and he saw the leggy redhead slide out of her booth and make her way toward them.

Carley groaned. "Told you," she complained under her breath.

"Well, well. If it isn't Sloan McKinney," Kimberly greeted, her voice as smooth as warm whiskey. "I heard you were back in town." She reached over and skimmed her index finger over his badge. "And you're a Texas Ranger now."

Sloan recognized that come-hither look in those familiar dove-gray eyes and he ignored it. He didn't have the time or the inclination to play around with Kimberly. "Carley and I are investigating Sarah Wallace's murder."

"Carley," Kimberly repeated. She aimed a weak, mechanical smile at Carley, but that smile warmed up considerably when she looked at him. "I'm an RN at Dr. Evans's clinic. Maybe you could stop by sometime?"

"I'm really tied up with the case."

Kimberly wasn't taking no for an answer. "*Try.* I'd love to see you and talk over old times."

Sloan gave her a vague nod so that she'd leave and then he had to face Carley's semiamused expression. "*Try,*" Carley repeated in a mock-sultry voice.

"Hey, what can I say? It's the Ranger outfit. It's a magnet for old flames."

"It's a magnet, period." She plucked a blueberry

from her stack of pancakes and popped it in her mouth. "In Texas, that badge is an aphrodisiac."

"Really?" He couldn't resist. "Is that why you applied to be a Ranger?"

The blueberry apparently lodged in her throat, because she sputtered out a cough. "How did you know about that?"

"My boss mentioned it because he noticed we were from the same town. He asked if I knew you."

The color drained from her face. "And what did you tell him?"

"The truth," Sloan said quickly just so she wouldn't lose any more color. "I told him that from what I'd heard, you'd been doing a great job in Justice. I mentioned that armed bank robber you nabbed, the one that was on the FBI's Most Wanted list."

"That collar was a fluke, not a testament to my skills as a law-enforcement officer. When the man tried to check into the inn, I recognized him from his Wanted poster." Carley waved off her accomplishment as if it were nothing. "Besides, being a Ranger is a pipe dream for me."

"Why?"

"You have to ask? Well, for one thing, I'm not presently a member of the Department of Public Safety."

"But you left your position only a few months ago. Before that, you were there for several years,"

Sloan reminded her. "Didn't you join not long after I became the deputy here in Justice?"

That brought some color back to her cheeks. "You mean the deputy job we competed for and you got? Yes, that one. Actually, I finished up my degree in criminal justice first and then applied to DPS. I also have my mandatory two years of duty at the department, but I'd still have to have a waiver to be a Ranger since I'm not presently working at DPS."

"A waiver like that could be approved," he insisted. "Especially since you have your degree and because you gave up your job with DPS to help out a town in need of a sheriff. Plus, you have a sterling record."

"I'm a small-town female rookie sheriff," Carley corrected. "I don't have a state baseball championship under my belt, I've never ridden in a rodeo and I'm not a good ole boy."

Sloan exaggerated a breath of relief. "Believe me, I'm thankful for that last part."

She frowned at him. "Be serious."

"Oh, I am being serious. We had that, uh, accident with our mouths bumping together. That wouldn't have happened if you'd been a boy."

"Very funny," she said with sarcasm, but her brief smile was genuine.

Sloan could have pressed for this to continue, he could have put her more at ease, but he knew that would be playing with fire. Carley and he needed solidarity between them to work together on this case, but they didn't need anything personal developing.

He repeated that to himself.

Several times.

"Uh-oh. There's Donna Hendricks," Carley mumbled.

Well, that got his mind back on business. "Is she coming over here, too?"

"No, I think she's trying to ignore us."

"Good. Maybe she'll continue to do that. I don't want to talk to her again until we've made some progress with Lou Ann's papers."

Carley covered her mouth with her hand and groaned softly. "She keeps glancing over here."

"Maybe that's because you keep glancing over there," he pointed out.

"Heck, here she comes. Act surprised so she won't think we were talking about her."

Sloan gave Carley a flat look. "What good would acting surprised possibly do?"

"I don't want her to know that we're talking about her or she'll probably feel cornered. I think it's best if she believes Leland is our number one suspect. That way Donna might open up more."

Well, it wasn't totally logical, but it had some merit. Donna was far friendlier than her ex. However, that wasn't saying much since Sloan always got the feeling that Donna's "nice moments" were a facade. "Still, she might provide us with something we can use to arrest Leland."

"That, too," Carley mumbled.

She stopped in front of their booth. "Carley. Sloan." It wasn't exactly a warm greeting, though she did have a shiny silver coffee carafe. It looked foreign in her hand, and Donna clutched it as if she'd never held something like a serving container.

Donna topped off both their cups, splashing more than a little onto the saucers. That whole pouring routine looked foreign, as well.

She glanced at Carley's stack of uneaten pancakes. "Maybe you'd like to try the quiche this morning? It's my grandmother's recipe, and I've been told that the chef does a decent job preparing it."

"No. Thanks."

Donna's glancing didn't stop with the pancakes. Her ever vigilant gaze drifted onto the papers lying in front of Carley. Her thin, overly tweezed eyebrows flexed slightly before she turned to Sloan. She smiled at him.

"I heard you were staying at the inn," Donna commented.

That statement seemed to be a fishing expedition. Sloan had no intention of providing her any real information. "For now."

"Well, I'm sure you'll be comfortable there. And you won't have to deal with all those pesky family issues." She turned to Carley. "One day I'll make the

Mathesons an offer they can't refuse, and they'll sell the inn to me."

"It isn't for sale," Carley volunteered.

"So you've said. But I have to keep trying, don't I? After all, it was my childhood home."

"It was my childhood home, too," Carley reminded her.

Donna's gaze drifted back to Sarah's papers, and Carley obviously noticed. She slid her arm over them. Sloan did the same to his.

That caused another eyebrow flex from Donna. "Well, if you change your mind about that quiche or selling the inn, just let me know. I have an office in the back and I'll be there all morning."

With that, Donna strolled away. Sloan watched her as she made her way toward the door that led into the kitchen. She stopped and said something to a tall, thin Hispanic woman who was about the same age as Donna.

"That's Rosa Ramirez," Carley supplied in a whisper.

Sloan watched the two women. "She was the nanny for Leland and Donna's son."

"Yes, and now she manages this diner for Donna. They've remained close."

"Obviously. Guess that's because Rosa used to buy booze and other things for Donna," Sloan surmised. "You've questioned her?"

"Not yet. Zane has, but I want to talk to her about

these pills and booze purchases. It was on my list of things to do."

It was on Sloan's list now.

Maybe the former nanny had some juicy details that would either confirm or deny Lou Ann's notes. If he could verify any of the information from another source, like a former nanny, then they might be able to use it to show Leland and Donna's criminal natures.

"We probably shouldn't be reading these papers here," Sloan suggested.

"I agree. Donna has prying eyes and she probably would love to know what her ex-husband's dead wife had to say about her." Carley gathered up her things and slipped them into her briefcase. "We can continue this in my office."

"Good idea." Sloan put his copies in his briefcase, as well, dropped some money on the table and stood.

"Thanks for buying me breakfast," Carley said when she faced him.

"You didn't eat breakfast," he pointed out.

"I wasn't very hungry."

She turned, and Sloan and she walked out of the diner together. He took one last glance at Donna and Rosa. They were still whispering about something. Oh, to be a fly on the wall of that conversation. Sloan wasn't convinced that either was guilty, but he darn sure wasn't convinced of their innocence, either.

Carley shifted her briefcase to her other hand. It was a simple maneuver, but it caught his attention.

"How's your side?" he asked. "Still hurting?"

"It's healing."

"So it's still hurting," he concluded.

Huffing, she returned the briefcase to her original hand. "I added double adhesive, so there'll be no reason for you to check my bandage today."

He snapped his fingers. "Darn it. Here, I was looking forward to it."

And unfortunately that had some truth in it. Too much truth.

She stopped and stared at him. "You know that nothing can happen between us, right?"

"Absolutely."

"Good. Because I know it, too."

She started to walk away, but he caught onto her arm. "You think our bodies know that nothing can happen?"

"They don't have a say in this." She shook off his grip and got moving. "Look, I have an idea how we can beat this…well, whatever this is. If our feelings start to soften for each other, then you just think of your father. Just remember that I'm the one who nearly sent him to jail."

It was a good idea. In theory. "And you'll think about how I beat you out for the deputy job."

She nodded. "That'll do it. I've stewed over that for years."

And he'd felt guilty for years. In fact, it was that guilt that'd caused him to apply to be a Ranger. It had apparently driven Carley to do the same.

Strange. How one event could change both their lives.

That got Sloan to thinking—how was that accidental kiss going to change things? And it had changed things all right. Sloan couldn't deny that. That meant when he left Justice and returned to his office, he would spend a lot of time trying to forget how memorable that kiss was.

Sloan could feel it even now. How her mouth had felt against his. Her scent.

Yes, her scent.

Carley didn't need perfume because there was something special about the way she smelled. Something that couldn't come from a bottle.

Beside him, Carley cursed softly.

"What's wrong?" he asked, pulling himself out of his rather heated fantasy.

"*Us*. That's what's wrong." She stopped again and turned to him. "Let's get something straight right now. I don't want you in my life. I want to do my job here and, if a miracle happens, someday I want to be a Ranger. I want to pour all my energy into that. Understand?"

"Totally. I don't want you in my life, either. And you don't have to worry. This stuff simmering between us is just lust. That's it. I saw something about it on the Science Channel. It's a scent-at-traction thing. Our DNAs are compatible and our bodies are sending off scents that draw us to each other. Our DNAs hope that we'll have some hot, mindless, stranded-on-a-deserted-island sex and produce offspring."

She looked at him as if he'd grown a third eye. "The Science Channel?"

It didn't sound any better coming from her. "Hey, I watch stuff other than cop shows and sports." Best to defuse the situation by changing the subject.

"I'll give you that. But *hot, mindless, stranded-on-a-deserted-island sex?*"

The corner of his mouth lifted. "I'm not even going to try to explain that."

"Good." Though, judging from the blush that crept over her cheeks, she was imagining it.

So was he.

Hell.

Just how was he supposed to cope with this?

"Carley?" someone called out.

That interruption was in the nick of time. Because heaven knows Sloan needed something to get his mind back on track.

The woman who stepped out of the Sew and Sew shop was Mildred Kerrville, the shop's septuagenarian owner and a woman that Sloan had known his entire life.

"Sloan, it's so good to see you. As good-looking

as ever. Both you McKinney boys sure got your daddy's looks." Mildred came up on her tiptoes and caught onto Sloan's chin so she could pull him down for a kiss on the cheek. "You say hello to your mama for me."

"I will." It was a polite lie that he'd told often over the years.

"I was just coming to find you, Carley," Mildred announced, ending it with a weary huff.

Carley glanced at Sloan before giving Mildred her full attention. "What can I do for you?"

"Well, you know I had that security camera installed just like you suggested after those kids spray painted bad words and graffiti all over the windows. I've got in the habit of looking at the tape while I'm having my morning coffee." She lowered her voice to a secretive whisper. "You'd be surprised how some people act when they don't know anyone is watching 'em."

"I know what you mean," Carley answered.

"The camera recorded something last night. You're not going to believe this." Mildred's violet-colored eyes danced with excitement.

In contrast, Carley's eyes were clear and focused. She was very much the cop now. "Try me."

"There was a car parked right out here, just a few yards from the shop's front door."

"Dark four-door?" Sloan asked. "The license plates covered with mud or something?"

Mildred nodded. "Yes, did you see it, too?"

"Carley did."

"Well, how about the goofy driver? What was that all about, huh?"

Carley and Sloan exchanged another glance. "I didn't see the driver. I take it you did?" Carley asked.

"Sort of. I mean, the camera recorded it. The person inside must have been dressed for a costume party or something, because he or she was wearing a black cloak."

Other than a quick breath, Carley had no external reaction, but Sloan knew that inside there was a lot of adrenaline and emotion.

"I'll need to take a look at that surveillance tape," Carley insisted.

"Sure. Figured you would. It might be one of those graffiti morons scoping out the place again." Mildred hurried back inside her shop, and several seconds later she reappeared with the tape in hand. She gave it to Carley.

"By any chance, did the camera happen to record the person's face?" Sloan asked.

"No. But you can see that cloak as clear as day. I'm talking a midnight-black cloak with a big ole hood. Just like what you'd wear on Halloween." Mildred shook her head. "What kind of person drives around wearing a getup like that in the dead heat of summer?"

Sloan knew the answer: a killer.

Specifically a killer who was after Carley.

Chapter Eight

"'After Mama got settled into the Matheson Inn that afternoon, she phoned me,'" Carley read aloud from the notes that Sarah had written. "'Mama told me she'd called Donna to tell her that Leland was planning to do a fake kidnapping and murder of little Justin so he could collect on the insurance policy.'"

Carley let that information percolate in her head. It wasn't the only thing percolating. It's been a long day with Sloan and her reviewing Mildred Kerrville's surveillance tape and going over the details of the murder investigations.

It would be a long night, too.

She set the page aside and stepped out from her bubble bath. Carley hated to leave the soothing, warm water, but she was smudging the copied pages with her now pruned fingers. Besides, she needed to redress her injury.

And she also needed to look out the window again.

Yes, look out the window.

That particular activity had become an obsession of sorts, and she saw no sense in denying it—to herself anyway. What she couldn't do was stop it from happening. She had this uncontrollable urge to see if someone was parked near the inn, watching her.

Waiting to take another shot.

Suddenly the obsession became overwhelming. Carley quickly dried off and went into her adjoining bedroom to locate some underwear. Best not to peer out windows while stark naked. She frowned, though, when she opened the drawer.

Purple silk panties, a pair of pink ones and two pink bras.

She made a mental note to do laundry, then put on the purple frilly panties and her well-worn green cotton bathrobe and she went to the window.

The street below was empty.

That was normal. After all, it was nearly 10:00 p.m. on a weeknight, and Justice wasn't exactly a hotbed for nightlife activity. Everyone was probably tucked inside their homes watching TV or already in bed.

"Only the paranoid are staring out windows," she mumbled, disgusted with herself.

Besides, the cloaked driver of that car probably wouldn't be ballsy enough for a return visit. Especially since it'd already gotten all over town that

Mildred Kerrville's security camera had filmed the person and the vehicle and that the surveillance tape was on the way to the Rangers' crime lab. Carley wasn't counting on the lab or the tape to provide them any information—other than the likelihood that a would-be killer wearing a cloak was playing mind games with her.

Sadly the mind games were working.

After all, she was staring out the window. Her anxiety level was sky-high. And she couldn't eat because her stomach was vised in a knot.

With that reminder, Carley snapped the curtains closed and forced herself back into the bathroom to retrieve the papers she'd been studying. While she was at it, she hurried to the kitchen and tossed a bag of popcorn into the microwave. By God, she was going to eat. And she wasn't looking out that window again tonight. She'd concentrate on doing her job because that and only that would stop the cloaked jerk from playing with her head.

Fortified by her mental lecture, she leaned against the kitchen counter and continued reading. Carley repeated what Sarah had written to force herself to regain focus.

Mama told me she'd called Donna to tell her that Leland was planning to do a fake kidnapping and murder of little Justin so he could collect on the insurance policy.

Okay. That helped Carley with her focusing problem. The immediate question that came to mind—was Lou Ann's call the first Donna had heard about the fake kidnapping or had she already known about it? If so, from whom?

Rosa Ramirez, the nanny, was a definite possibility.

That made sense. Rosa and Donna were friendly with each other, and Donna seemed to trust the woman to buy her pills and booze, along with entrusting Rosa with the care of her beloved toddler son. So maybe Rosa had learned about Leland's sinister plan and she told Donna.

Then what?

Carley scanned down the page and flipped to the next one. She had to make it through several paragraphs before she found what she was looking for.

According to Sarah:

Mama told Donna that she'd put a stop to Leland's plan and help her get back her little boy if Donna was willing to pay up. Donna was trying hard to get the cash together but wasn't having a lot of luck. Mama knew Donna had the money, so she told her to get it and get it fast or the deal was off. Donna said she would but that after she gave Mama the money, Mama was to call the FBI and turn in Leland for his fake kidnapping plan.

"Why?" Carley asked herself.

If Donna knew about the fake kidnapping, then why didn't she go to the police or the FBI herself? It would have been cheaper and less complicated. Heck, Donna could have even turned in Lou Ann for attempted extortion.

Carley played around with that question and scenario while she waited for the popcorn to be ready. Unfortunately there were a couple of possible answers for Donna to have planned what Lou Ann said she had planned. Donna might have wanted to remain one step removed from the fake-kidnapping mess with the hopes that she could regain custody of her son once Leland was arrested. If Donna had reported the possible crime, the sheriff or the FBI might have thought she was involved. This way Donna kept her hands clean.

Of course, maybe Donna couldn't go to the police because she didn't have any solid proof? Perhaps the nanny didn't either. Unlike some of his other dirty dealings, maybe Leland hadn't left memos and notes lying around. So the women might have had information but nothing to back it up. With Leland's power and influential friends, they would definitely have needed something to back it up.

So did that mean Lou Ann had proof?

"Maybe not physical proof," Carley said, talking it out loud. The microwave dinged, indicating that the popcorn was ready, but she ignored it and continued. "But Leland had told Lou Ann that he wanted her to help him carry out the fake kidnapping. And maybe Lou Ann was the only person he'd told directly."

Carley bobbed her head. Yep. That fit. Leland would have wanted as few people as possible to be able to link him to this crime. Lou Ann was probably the one who could, even if that was only through unrecorded conversation.

Carley continued reading, and her attention stopped dead when she came to Sarah's next account.

Leland didn't have a clue that Donna was going to pay Mama or that Mama was thinking about turning him in to the FBI. Mama said if Leland found out, the crap would hit the fan and God knows what he would do.

Ah. Carley understood now. It was a classic double cross. Lou Ann let Leland believe she would go through with the fake kidnapping and equally fake murder, but behind the scenes Lou Ann was trying to milk Donna for money. It was entirely likely that once Lou Ann had Donna's money, she would leave town and not go through with either of her promises: to assist Leland or to help Donna get her son back.

Carley's eyes widened when she saw the amount that Lou Ann claimed Donna was willing to pay her.

Five hundred thousand dollars.

That wasn't chump change.

So where had Donna gotten the money?

"There could be a money paper trail," Carley practically shouted.

A paper trail could tell them something critical: timing. How close to Lou Ann's murder had Donna scraped the funds together? Or had Donna even managed it? Maybe she hadn't been able to get the money after all. Or if she had, maybe Donna hadn't managed to gather the funds until after Lou Ann was murdered. If so, that would go a long way to clearing Donna's name and implicating the heck out of Leland.

This might be the break they'd been looking for. And if so, Sloan needed to know that ASAP.

Carley considered calling his room, but this was better done face-to-face, so she hugged the papers to her chest and hurried out the door. She was out of breath by the time she'd raced down the stairs and reached his room, but she didn't even take the time to steady herself. She knocked and then knocked again when he didn't immediately answer.

The door finally opened, and Carley held up the papers. "I think I found something."

Sloan stood there, papers and copied notes in his own hand. She hardly noticed that he had on only one item of clothing—loose jeans that rode low on his hips. No shirt, just a rather toned and tanned bare chest that was sprinkled with dark coils of hair.

Okay, so she noticed.

But Carley ignored it.

Because a man's hot body was minor compared to getting a break in this case.

"There might be a paper trail for the money that Donna intended to pay Lou Ann," she proudly announced. "And the timing of that trail could help nail Leland Hendricks."

"Yes. I just realized that, too. I was about to get dressed and come up to tell you."

Oh.

Well, that put a damper on her elation.

"You said we were going to work together when going over these papers," Carley challenged.

He lifted his eyebrow to indicate she hadn't exactly followed that rule either.

"Point taken," she grumbled. But she quickly dismissed her dampered excitement. "I can get a search warrant for all of Donna's financial records."

"Zane can get one faster. I just left a message for him on his cell phone." He shut the door, reached out and adjusted her robe.

Only then did Carley realize that a great deal of her right breast was exposed. Nipple and all.

Sheez.

Judging from the sudden tightness in Sloan's jaw and the fire she saw in those blue eyes, it'd had an effect on him, too. Not good. She hadn't subconsciously come here to get hot and bothered.

Honestly.

And she meant it.

Really.

"Sorry," she said. "I've been so obsessed with other things that I still haven't done laundry."

The tightness in his jaw got worse. "Does that mean you're not wearing panties, either?"

Because the inflection in his voice didn't change, it took a moment for that to sink in. And, boy, did it sink in. It was a massive understatement, but Carley was beginning to regret this visit.

"I have on panties," she snarled. "And you need to get your mind back on business. For starters, how about putting on a shirt?"

That seemed to amuse him or something. His mouth quivered, threatening a smile. Still, he strolled across the room, took the white shirt that'd been draped over the back of a chair and eased it on. What he didn't do was button it.

Great.

Somehow that made him look hotter than being totally shirtless. The open fabric only accentuated his washboard abs. Before she could suppress the thought, she wondered how it might feel to run her fingers over his…

"How soon can you start bugging Zane about getting that search warrant?" she asked, interrupting that thought because it desperately needed interrupting.

He seemed a little puzzled with her brusque tone. "I was going to call him again in about ten minutes."

Good. They were on the same page of urgency. But maybe they weren't on the same page for other things, like this crazy attraction. She could only wish that Sloan was saner about this than she was.

Again Carley forced herself to stay focused on the case. "I just hope that, after all this time, Donna hasn't been able to hide the trail."

He shrugged, though his eyes conveyed no such casualness. He was staring at her. "That's not an easy thing to hide. I'm going to ask Zane to have that search warrant cover Rosa Ramirez's records, as well."

Surprised, Carley stared at him. "You don't think she gave Donna that kind of money?"

"No. If Rosa had bucks like that, she probably wouldn't have been working for Leland Hendricks. But maybe Donna used Rosa to try to cover her tracks. A sort of money filtering through Rosa's accounts. We might have to do a lot of digging to get to the source of that cash, especially if Donna is our killer and took extreme measures to cover up what she was doing."

And there was no doubt about it—a killer would take those kinds of measures. "Still, it's a chance to get some concrete evidence, and we're seriously lacking that."

"We're closer than you might think. After all, someone is trying to eliminate you, and my gut tells me that it's related to the case. That means we must be getting close, and someone is terrified of that."

Carley nodded. It was true, but it wasn't much comfort. Still, thinking about this was far better than the alternative. It got her mind off his shirtless status and his abs. Unfortunately her mind went straight to the other topic she'd been trying not to think about: the attempts to end her life.

"Just how little sleep are you getting at night?" Sloan asked.

She frowned, not pleased that he'd apparently picked up on some body language that she hadn't wanted to convey. "I rarely sleep well when I'm this involved in a case."

He blew out a weary breath. "And I suspect that's especially true after everything else that's happened. I would recommend that you go on a vacation—"

"Forget it."

"That's why I won't recommend it. So the next thing I won't recommend is that you try to relax."

"How?" But Carley tried to wave off her question when she realized how it might have sounded.

And it just might have sounded suggestive.

"You could relax by reminding yourself that you're not going to do anything stupid, like setting yourself up as bait again," Sloan suggested. "You're going to keep at this investigation until the person is caught. In other words, you're already doing everything you can do. And you'll let me help you do the rest."

It was reassuring. Why? Because it was coming from Sloan. And that set off loud alarms in her head.

"I shouldn't have come here to your room," she mumbled.

"You got caught up in the excitement of the case." Another breath. This one was short and tense. "You forgot that I was a man."

The room suddenly got warmer. A *lot* warmer. And why had the air simply vanished? There definitely wasn't enough air in her lungs.

"I could never forget that you're a man. What I forgot about was the strength of this attraction," she corrected.

This time his breath seemed to stop. "You're admitting that?"

"It would seem stupid not to admit it. Though, in hindsight, I wish I hadn't," she added when she noted the change in him. Heat sizzled through his eyes, and she could see the muscles in his chest and stomach flicker.

Carley had to do some backpedaling. Fast.

"I think the only reason I want you is because of that whole forbidden-fruit thing," she commented after she cleared her throat.

He shook his head. "Now I'm fruit?"

Carley nodded. And she kept a straight face. "The forbidden kind."

Though some of the puzzlement returned, it didn't soften his expression. In fact, nothing about him seemed to be softening. She, on the other hand, couldn't say the same. Her body seemed to be doing just that—softening. It was preparing itself for something it wasn't going to get.

It wasn't going to get Sloan McKinney.

He took a step toward her, reached and skimmed his finger down her cheek. "And what about when you were a teenager? I wasn't forbidden fruit then."

Because her body seemed to be making yet more preparations, she stepped away from his skimming finger, which seemed to have the ability to ignite all her erogenous zones with one single stroke.

"That doesn't count," she managed to say. "And it doesn't count now. In addition to forbidden fruit, you're an adrenaline reaction. That's it. Nothing more. A reaction to danger." She frowned when he smiled. "Hey, it's better than your Science Channel DNA explanation."

Sloan retraced that step toward her. His shirt shifted, sliding against his bare skin. She could hear it.

Heck, she could *feel* it.

"In just a couple of seconds I'm going to kiss you," he announced. "If it'll make you feel better, you can act surprised."

Carley swallowed hard and slapped her hand on his chest. "There's no need to act surprised, because it's not going to happen. Think this through, Sloan. You're still my boss. I'm not having sex with my boss."

"Carley, no one said anything about having sex." His voice dropped to that low, sexy drawl that was an aphrodisiac in itself.

"Kissing leads to sex eventually. In our case, eventually wouldn't be long at all. Minutes. Heck, who am I kidding? It'd lead to sex in seconds. And if someone were to find out, it'd hurt your career and it'd ruin any chances I have of becoming a Ranger."

"You're right, of course." Sloan reached out, skimmed his thumb over her bottom lip, sending a hot shiver through her. "But then, no one has to find out, do they?"

No, they didn't.

But Carley knew that was rationalizing.

"You and I would know," she pointed out.

He nodded. "If we do it right, yes, we'll know. That's the way a good kiss works."

She laughed. Not from humor. Definitely not. But from nerves that were already too close to the surface. "Why does that suddenly seem so tempting that I'm not sure I want to resist?" she asked, only partly sarcastic. "Oh. I know why." She tried to put some steel in her voice. "Because I've lost my mind, that's why."

"You haven't lost your mind, Carley. I've lost mine." And with that, he dipped his head and kissed her.

Until his mouth touched hers, Carley had been prepared to argue, to step away, to leave. But that kiss—*wow,* that kiss. It changed everything. Sloan was very good at it, and she went from thinking about that argument to thinking about nothing else but him.

Carley didn't resist when he hooked his arm around her waist and eased her closer to him. Nope. Nor did she resist when he cupped her neck with the palm of his hand. Or when his body pressed against hers. Ditto on a no-protest reaction when Sloan deepened the kiss and turned it into long, slow and French.

In fact, Carley did the opposite of resisting.

She lifted her arms. First one. Then the other. And she put them around him. She let the silky heat slide through her body. She let the kiss consume her. Not that it was difficult for that to happen. Oh, no. Sloan had a way of monopolizing time, space and thought with his mouth.

He tasted the way he smelled. Not specifically like his manly aftershave, but there it was again— summer picnics, the woods. And sex.

Definitely the sex.

The feel of his body pushing against her had a unique way of making her dwell on the sex, too. Probably because that's exactly what she wanted from him—sex—and her body was starting to clamor that it wanted it now.

She'd been right and wrong about the kiss. The right part was because she'd said it could lead to sex within minutes. Seconds, even. But she'd been wrong about the intensity. Of course, nothing could have prepared her for that.

Carley let him claim her mouth while she took every ounce of pleasure from him. They fit together. Her soft breasts against his hard chest. The sensation against her bare skin shocked her for a moment. Then she realized her robe had come open, and with his already opened shirt, his chest hair was tickling her nipples. She'd never considered just how pleasurable that would feel, but she considered it now.

Better yet, she savored it.

Sloan eased back a bit and slid his hand between them. Specifically he slid his hand over her right breast. Yet more pleasure. But the slight shift in their positions allowed her to make eye contact. In the swirls of all that blue fire, she could see the struggle he was having with himself.

Oh, yes.

Definitely a struggle.

It was a struggle that Carley figured she should be having, as well. Because the arguments were still there. He was her boss. This could cause them to lose focus. But the most important reason of all was because she wasn't willing to risk her heart. Not like this.

Not to Sloan.

Even if by some miracle they could get beyond their past, their futures and their destinies were not on the same course. When this case was solved, he'd leave Justice, and kisses and sex would be long forgotten.

At least on his part.

Carley didn't think she would forget any of this, ever.

She fought her way through the thick, sensual haze. Through the pleasure that his kisses and touches were giving her. And she had to fight hard. She had to override all those primal instincts that were telling her it was time to give herself to this man.

"If we keep this up," she said, her breath thin and choppy, "we'll do something both of us will regret—we'll have sex. I really have to get out of here."

Carley backed up her insistence with some real action. She stepped back, closed her robe and tightened the sash. While she was on a sanity-saving, career-salvaging roll, she grabbed her copies of Lou Ann's papers and rushed out the door.

She had to put some space between Sloan and her. She had to think. And Carley figured when she was done with that thinking she'd be glad that she'd ended that kiss before things got carried away.

But she wasn't glad about it now.

No.

Her body was begging her to go back and take everything that Sloan McKinney was offering. And judging from those kisses, he could offer a lot.

Carley actually stopped halfway down the hall. Stopped. Cursed. Pleaded with herself to do the right thing. And the right thing was to return to her apartment. Somehow she mustered enough willpower to get her feet moving again.

It was too little, too late.

She heard the movement behind her, turned and saw a very determined-looking Sloan storming right for her.

Chapter Nine

Sloan only had a ten-second debate with himself before he grabbed his holster and went after Carley. He knew, depending on how this played out, it could be one of the best ideas he'd ever had.

Or the absolute worst.

Still, he had to risk it. Because it didn't matter what was or wasn't happening between them personally, he still had a job to do.

Carley was part of that job.

A big part. He didn't want anyone taking another shot at her. In addition to the obvious danger of something like that, it would pretty much destroy what little peace of mind she had left.

He caught up with Carley in the hall not too far from his room, but judging from her deer-caught-in-headlights expression, she wasn't happy to see him.

Well, he wasn't exactly happy with himself, either.

Only minutes earlier he'd let a certain part of his

body do his thinking for him and Sloan knew for a fact that part of him rarely made good decisions.

"Oh, no." Carley shook her head and backed away from him. "Turn around and go back to your room. There'll be no more kissing."

"No more kissing," he promised.

He strapped on his waist holster and buttoned his shirt. It wouldn't look good if anyone were to see them. Especially since Carley was wearing only her bathrobe. He could perhaps justify one of them being half-dressed but not both of them.

Though there was no way he'd be able to justify to anyone that just-kissed look of Carley's slightly swollen, damp mouth. Her face was still flushed with arousal.

And Sloan reacted to her arousal.

He felt that kick of lust and bit his bottom lip to stave it off. This was not the time for sex-against-the-wall thoughts about Carley.

"No more kissing," he repeated, hoping that his body grasped the ultimatum he'd just given it.

Carley ran her gaze down him from head to toe, and Sloan prayed that she wasn't disappointed with that ultimatum. Both of them had to stay rational here or they were going to lose this battle.

"Then if you're not here to resume the kiss, what are you doing here in the hall?" she asked.

He made a show of buttoning his shirt. "What does it look like I'm doing?"

Carley cocked her head to the side. "Asking for more trouble?"

"Perhaps." And heaven knows that was the truth. "But my number one motive is to make sure you get safely to your apartment."

"You're serious?" Oh, she did sound skeptical.

"As serious as my aunt Mary's quadruple bypass surgery."

She obviously didn't care much for his attempt to add some humor to this powder keg of a situation. She huffed, and with the papers hugged against her chest, she put her other hand on her hip. "Think this through—do you really want the temptation of following me to my bedroom?"

Sloan considered her lack of undergarments for a moment and then banished the thought from his head. "No. But I want to make sure you get there in one piece and that you lock the door behind you."

"Oh, I'll definitely arrive there in one piece since it's only one floor up. Hardly a long, dangerous trek behind enemy lines. And as soon as I'm there, I'll lock the door," she promised.

"And I'll listen to you do it." She obviously didn't approve of that, either, because Sloan had to catch onto her arm to stop her from walking away from him. "Trust me, this isn't special treatment because you're a woman. Or because I still want to kiss you. Or even because I don't think you can take care of yourself. *You can.* But I'd do this for anyone who works with me."

"So would I." She stayed quiet a moment. "But that means we're at a stalemate."

"How do you figure that?"

"Because after you've followed me to my apartment, I'll have to do what any good sheriff would do and then follow you back to your room to make sure all is well. If that happens, neither of us is going to get any sleep tonight."

"You won't follow me," Sloan insisted. Because heaven knows he couldn't go through another round of being alone and close with Carley. His willpower was nothing but dust now. "You'll go to your apartment and get some rest. What you won't do is spend the night worrying or digging through Lou Ann's papers."

The corner of her mouth lifted. "Does that mean you won't dig through them, either?"

Of course he would.

She would do the same.

Sloan smiled.

But his smile was short-lived.

Sloan's hand shot up in the air to cut off anything else she was about to say. But his hand alert wasn't necessary because Carley went dead quiet. She'd obviously heard the small, soft sound, as well. It had come from around the corner at the end of the hall.

Normally such a sound wouldn't have caused him to go on full alert, but then, there was nothing normal about this situation.

"Another guest?" he mouthed.

"Maybe. But I think there's only one other person staying on this floor."

So it was possible those were the legitimate footsteps of someone who had a right to be there. Still…

"Maybe it's someone on staff?" he suggested, speaking as softly as he could.

"No. The only person on duty is at the desk, and he wouldn't bother to get off his butt and come back here. Maintenance calls and such would go through me first and then I'd arrange for someone to come out." She paused. "Of course, it could be a late-night visitor."

That was possible, of course. But the feeling in the pit of Sloan's stomach said otherwise. He eased his gun from its holster.

Carley's eyes widened. "You think it's the killer?" she whispered.

"I don't want to take any chances."

Another nod. This one was choppy. He tried to give her a reassuring look and was certain he failed.

"Do you happen to have your cell phone with you?" Sloan asked.

Almost frantically she searched through the pockets of her robe. "No. You?"

He shook his head and tried not to curse out loud. Hell. How could he have forgotten something as important as that? Oh, yeah. He remembered. His brain was too occupied and too clouded because he'd had his mouth and hands all over Carley. Well, maybe this would teach him to keep the personal stuff away from a case.

Both waited.

Listening.

Sloan braced himself for more footsteps or something worse, but he hadn't braced himself for being plunged into total darkness.

Just like that.

The electricity went out.

Or, more likely, someone had cut the power.

He felt Carley move and he caught onto her arm to make sure she stayed put. Her cop instincts were probably screaming for her to investigate what had just happened. His instincts were doing the same. But Sloan had an even greater instinct for survival, and everything inside him was telling him to keep still until they could figure out what was going on. The darkness would cloak them.

Unfortunately it could cloak a killer, as well.

The thought had no sooner crossed his mind when he heard more footsteps.

Because Carley was so close, he felt her body tense. Her breath thinned. And Sloan knew why.

Those footsteps were headed up the back stairs to the third floor. And there was only one thing up there.

Carley's apartment.

Chapter Ten

Sloan's eyes slowly adjusted to the darkness. Because this particular section of the hall didn't have any windows, there was no help from the streetlights. Still, he could discern inanimate objects from humans.

He hoped.

Just in case his night vision was off, he tightened his grip on Carley's arm and eased her behind him. She didn't protest, thank God, but then, she wasn't armed. It was a good thing he'd brought his weapon with him or else they'd have no way to protect themselves.

"Any idea who'd be going up to your apartment?" he whispered.

"No. I'm not expecting anyone."

He was afraid she would say that.

Sloan was about to suggest that she go back to his room, lock the door and wait there—just until he checked things out—but he doubted Carley would agree to that. Plus, it might not be the safe thing to do. After all, he didn't have any other weapons in the inn, and that meant he'd be sending her back alone in the darkness without any way to defend herself. At least if she stayed near him he would be able to take care of her.

Something Carley definitely wouldn't have liked.

Still, what choice did they have? If there was indeed a would-be killer headed up to Carley's apartment, it was their sworn duty to intercept and hopefully arrest the person. In fact, this could turn out to be a good thing. Once they got past the danger, that is. Sloan didn't like putting Carley in harm's way, especially since she was still recovering from her injuries.

"We can't just stand here all night. Let's go," she mumbled. "I want to catch this monster."

Sloan got moving when Carley nudged him with her elbow, but he made sure he stayed firmly in front of her. It earned him a huff, but he didn't care. Their positions were not negotiable.

He took it slowly, one quiet step at a time, and he kept his gun aimed and ready—just in case the person came barreling back down the stairs. However, with each step the adrenaline sped through him, his heart pounded harder and the questions came just as hard and fast.

For starters, how had the person cut the electricity?

Sloan figured there was a circuit-breaker box

somewhere, but how many people would have known where it was? Of course, it wouldn't have been difficult to find the location in a town the size of Justice. Heck, the dull-witted desk clerk who seemed to have headphones implanted into his ears might have voluntarily given up that information.

The next question was why was this person here? It was something Sloan had already given some thought. If this was related to Sarah's murder, then it all came right back to Carley. Maybe she hadn't seen anything specifically, but the killer might not believe that.

Sloan felt Carley move to the side and, fearing she might be ready to strike out ahead of him, he nearly grabbed her again. Then he realized she was taking the fire extinguisher from the wall.

"Good idea," he whispered.

It might come in handy as a backup weapon. Too bad they might need it before this was over.

Sloan eased Carley closer to the wall until she was pressed against it, and they continued their trek through the darkness. He tried to listen for the sound of more of those footsteps, but all he could hear was Carley's and his movement. But then, it was entirely possible that the person was already in Carley's apartment.

That was a sobering reminder.

Because if this was the killer, once he or she realized Carley wasn't there, he or she would be coming back down those stairs.

Right at them.

Except Sloan would be ready. Still, things could go wrong, and both Carley and he had experienced that firsthand.

Sloan stopped at the foot of the stairs and he pulled Carley into a recessed area next to a huge fernlike potted plant.

She leaned closer and put her mouth right against his ear. "I could go to the front desk and use the phone to call for backup."

It was tempting, but Sloan immediately saw a problem with that suggestion. For Carley to get to the front desk, she'd have to walk through at least twenty feet of a pitch-black hall, go downstairs, turn down an equally dark corridor and then go another twenty feet or so to the desk.

"Too risky," Sloan mumbled. "Is there any way the person can leave other than using these stairs?"

"Only through the window."

And he doubted the killer was willing to jump three stories to the ground.

So that meant they had to wait it out. Not the easiest thing he'd ever done. Especially with Carley beside him. Because with every passing second he became more and more aware of just how much danger she was in. If they didn't make an arrest *tonight,* he really had to do something to put an end to this. It couldn't continue.

Just when he thought his stomach couldn't

possibly take any more waiting, Sloan heard the sound.

Definitely footsteps.

He actually welcomed them. The person had probably already gone through Carley's apartment and was now trying to make a hasty exit.

Sloan wasn't about to let that happen.

"Stay put," he warned Carley.

He ignored her mumbled protest and stepped out of the recessed area so he'd have better position. The footsteps continued. Slow and cautious. This person obviously didn't want to be heard.

Sloan finally spotted the shadowy figure about a third of the way from the top of the steps. The person was still a little too far away for him to identify himself as a Texas Ranger and demand that the person halt. Sloan didn't want him or her to have time to turn and run. He definitely didn't need a chase through a dark inn, especially with an unarmed Carley in tow.

The figure took another step.

Then another.

Sloan made sure his aim was ready and dead-on and he opened his mouth to order the person to halt. But opening his mouth was as far as he got. He saw no shift of movement on the stairs, but he heard the sound.

A swish.

Like someone blowing out a candle.

However, the next sound followed a split second later, and it wasn't so soft. Something slammed into the wall only inches from where they stood.

A bullet.

Hell! The person had shot at them.

Sloan automatically hooked his arm around Carley to drag her to the floor. She went willingly, probably because she was familiar with that sound. The person had used a gun rigged with a silencer.

Another shot.

This one smacked into the stair railing and sent a spray of splinters in every direction. Sloan ducked his head to keep his eyes from being injured and came up prepared to fire. Unfortunately so did the other person.

There was another shot, and it came so close to them that Sloan could have sworn he felt the heat of the bullet on his cheek. This one tore into the plant.

He had no choice but to push Carley back against the meager protection of the stair casings and shield her with his body. It was a pitiful plan, mainly because it gave the shooter a chance to get down the steps.

And that's exactly what happened.

The footsteps were frantic now, and each one seemed to be punctuated with another shot. When the person reached the bottom of the stairs, Sloan knew he had to make his move.

But he couldn't.

The next shot missed his head by a fraction of an inch.

He stayed down, counting off the seconds and listening as the person ran out the back exit. Then he did what he had to do. Yelling for Carley to stay put, he hurried to the door. He had his wrist braced with his hand so he could control his aim and fire.

But no one was there in the tiny parking lot at the back of the inn. Beyond it, though, there was movement in the trees.

Sloan cursed. He couldn't take a blind shot and risk hurting an innocent bystander. He also couldn't go racing into the woods after the person. It'd be suicide, since the gunman could be hiding behind one of the massive oaks in the woods, just waiting for Sloan to appear so he or she could gun him down.

"What's happening?" Carley called out.

He really hated to be the bearer of bad news, but there was no way around this. "They got away."

With the papers and fire extinguisher still in her hands, Carley rushed toward him. "Are you okay?"

"Fine." That was close to the truth, anyway. "How about you?"

"I'm furious," she snarled. She practically threw the fire extinguisher to the floor. "And I'm sick and tired of this. I'm going to front desk to call for backup. I want those woods searched."

"And I'll call Zane. Whoever it was in your room might have left fingerprints." He kept his attention staked to the thick woods in case the person made a return visit.

"We have to catch this person, Sloan." She sounded desperate. And probably was. He was certainly to the point of feeling that way.

"We will." He tensed when a tree branch moved slightly but then felt the breeze. Hell. The man or woman who fired those shots was long gone. "We know more now of what we're dealing with. This person can shoot."

Of course, that didn't rule out any of their suspects. All of them could shoot. In fact, both Donna and Leland had permits to carry concealed weapons.

"Whoever did this knew the layout of the inn," Carley mumbled.

Sloan nodded, furious with himself that he hadn't thought of that sooner. "Yes. I'm sure Leland's visited the place enough over the years."

"He worked here when he was a teenager."

Sloan recalled people talking about that. But it wasn't Leland that concerned him the most right now.

It was Donna.

Since the inn was her childhood home. She would have known the location of the box for the circuit breaker, the safest place to enter and exit and how many steps to Carley's apartment. She would have known every creaky board to avoid on the stairs.

"Come on," he told Carley. "Let's check on the desk clerk and then make that call to Zane. I want Donna Hendricks brought in for questioning. One way or another, this ends *now*."

Chapter Eleven

Carley thanked Luis, the deputy, for the cup of coffee that he handed her. Once the deputy was out of her office and sight, she set the cup next to the still uneaten breakfast taco that Luis had brought in a half hour earlier. She wasn't interested in food or drink.

Or the uncustomary sympathy that Luis was showing her.

She was only interested in the latest phone conversation that Sloan was having with his brother, Zane. This call had to give them answers because heaven knows they were seriously lacking in that area. It's been more than eight hours since the attempt to kill them and she was tired of waiting. Heck, she was just tired, period.

Thankfully, no one had been physically hurt in the attack. Including the desk clerk. Sloan and she had checked on the teenager almost immediately afterward and found him practicing some dance moves to the music pouring through his headphones. In addition to being unharmed, he was also oblivious to the fact there'd been a shooting. He hadn't seen or heard anything, except his favorite group's latest lyrics.

Sloan slapped his phone shut and looked at her. "Zane says that unless we get a rock-solid confession from either Leland, Donna or both, we can't make an arrest," he explained, his voice weary with fatigue and spent adrenaline.

"So what do we do?" Carley asked, her own voice as weary as Sloan's.

"I know it's not what you want to hear—it's not what I want to hear, either—but we need to let the grand jury continue to do what they're doing. If they come back with a verdict that there's enough evidence, then we can do what we're both itching to do—get Leland and Donna behind bars."

Carley listened to Sloan's summary of the chat he'd just finished with his brother, and it didn't take her long to realize that it wasn't a summary she liked.

"Neither Leland nor Donna will confess," she concluded. "There's too much at stake."

"True. But one of them might slip up." Sloan sat on the edge of her desk, cupped her chin and lifted it to force eye contact. "The person who fired at us is as bold as brass. People like that make mistakes. And the biggest mistake of all was coming into the inn. It's hard to come into a place and not leave a piece of yourself behind as evidence."

Since the chin cupping and the softly drawled explanation seemed a little too close for comfort, Carley rolled her chair back a few inches to break the physical contact. "Have the crime-scene guys found any prints in my apartment?"

Sloan shook his head. "The doorknob was wiped clean. But that doesn't mean there aren't other prints," he quickly added. "Or fibers or hair strands or some other trace evidence that we can use to ID this person."

It was a long shot, though, especially since the shooter had taken the time to wipe away the prints on the doorknob. That meant the gunman had almost certainly taken even more precautions.

"What about gunshot residue?" Carley asked.

Another head shake from Sloan. "We don't know yet. Both Donna's and Leland's hands were swabbed last night, right after they were brought in. We should have the results in an hour or so."

Of course, gunshot residue could be nullified simply by the shooter wearing gloves and disposing of the clothing that'd been worn during the attack. Carley was betting that neither Donna nor Leland had kept that black robe lying around for the police to find. *If* either was the culprit.

"You're still shaken up about the shooting," Sloan commented.

She didn't even bother to deny it. "Don't worry, it won't affect my job."

He groaned softly. "Carley—"

"Don't." She interrupted because that groan sounded like the start of a lecture to convince her to skip this interrogation. She wasn't skipping anything—especially this. If Donna Hendricks was out to kill her, then, by God, Carley wanted to go face-to-face with the woman.

Carley glanced across the hall and into the tiny interrogation room where Donna was sitting with her back to them.

Calmly sitting.

As if she didn't have a care in the world.

That didn't mean she was innocent. Nope. It just meant she was cool under pressure, but Carley hadn't needed this incident to know that. Unlike the frequently hotheaded Leland, Donna was much harder to read.

"By the way," Sloan said, closing the door so that it cut off Carley's view of Donna. He kept his voice at a whisper since there was nothing soundproof about the police station and he obviously didn't want Donna to hear them. "Neither Donna nor Leland have alibis for last night."

Well, that was interesting, and Carley didn't know whether to be pleased or more riled at the two. "How did you learn that?"

"While the deputies were processing the crime scene, Zane called them both within a half hour of the shooting. Neither was home. Leland's maid said he'd gone out for a drive—alone."

"And what about Donna?" Carley asked.

"All Zane got was her answering machine. When he realized she wasn't home, he had one of the deputies stake out her house, and she didn't get back in until nearly 3:00 a.m. When the deputy asked where she'd been, she refused to answer."

"Well, she'd better have an answer this morning," Carley grumbled. And then it hit her. "Why did Zane have one of the deputies stake out Donna's place? That's something I should have done."

"No, you couldn't have because you were in my room resting."

Oh, that did not sit well with her at all. "I wasn't resting. You imprisoned me in your room and wouldn't let me leave. I should have been doing that stakeout. I should have been doing something to catch the shooter."

"If you had done that, what good would you be to me this morning? I need someone to help me interrogate Leland and Donna. That wouldn't be a piece of cake under normal circumstances, but it'll be even more trying since we're interviewing them together."

She felt her eyes widen. "Together?"

"Yep." He checked his watch. "Leland should be here any minute. If not, I'll send someone out to bring him in."

Carley leaned back in her chair. "Why did you decide to do it this way?"

"Because I want to see if I can rattle them." He flashed a sly smile.

She certainly wasn't smiling. "That's not standard procedure," Carley pointed out.

"Standard procedure hasn't us gotten anywhere. It's time to try something they won't be expecting. They might find it hard to point fingers at each other if they're sitting side by side. Plus, we might get lucky and they might get into a no-holds-barred argument. Think of what they might say during the heat of the moment."

Carley did think about it, and that nearly brought out a smile. "Your plan has some merit."

"Glad you think so, because we need to decide how we're going to play this. I figured you could be the good cop. I'll be bad."

"Why?"

"Why what?"

"Why do you get to be bad?" she asked.

He exaggerated an eye roll. "Because I'm the Texas Ranger, the one who can arrest their guilty butts, and they know that. You can pretend to be somewhat protective of them, since you're their sheriff. Plus, you think they're innocent because you believe my father is guilty."

Sloan said it with such conviction that she almost denied it. Even more, she felt that denial in her heart. Mercy. After holding on to the belief of Jim's guilt for all these years, it didn't feel natural for her feelings to change, even a little. But she did seem to have a different attitude.

"I'm keeping an open mind about who's guilty of Lou Ann's and Sarah's murders," Carley told him. "And the attempts to kill us."

He hitched his thumb toward the interrogation room. "They don't know that."

Sloan was right, and they could perhaps use that to their advantage. "Okay. You win again. You're bad. I'm good."

There was a rap at the door, and a second later it opened. Deputy Luis Spinoza stuck his head inside. "Leland Hendricks is here."

"Thanks," Sloan answered. But he blocked Carley's way when she started to get up. He also waited for the deputy to leave before he continued. "One more thing—if I bring up anything from Lou Ann's notes and copied papers, whether it's true or not, I want you to act surprised."

She tried but couldn't think of a good reason to do that. "Why?"

"Because that way they'll believe you don't have access to the evidence."

Nothing could have stopped her from huffing or coming out of her chair. "You're trying to protect me. It won't work. I'm not acting surprised."

Sloan caught onto her shoulders, Carley tried to sidestep him, and they ended up doing an awkward dance. "It could save your life," he reminded her.

"And it'll make me look like an idiot, like someone who doesn't have a clue about what's happening in my own department."

"No. It'll make you look like a sheriff whose authority has been usurped by the Rangers. In addition to giving you some possible protection, it'll also help build that sheriff-citizen bond with Leland and Donna. We need that bond so they'll feel they can turn to you if one of them decides to rat out the other."

"A bond?" She stopped the dance by pushing him, hard, against the back of the door. It wasn't an ideal position, since she landed against Sloan. Body-to-body contact. Which she ignored. "That's BS."

"Maybe." Practically off-balancing her, he used his weight to reverse their positions. Her back went against the door. Sloan used his body to pin her in place. He got right in her face. "But I've already told you that I'll do whatever it takes to keep you safe. So, Carley, act surprised if I say anything about Lou Ann's papers. Deal?"

"No." She squirmed to break the lock he had on her. Not a good idea. His chest brushed against her breasts, creating a very unwelcome sizzling sensation. She must have rubbed him the wrong way, as well, because he sucked in his breath.

"*No* in this case is not an option," Sloan said. Though how he managed to talk with his jaw that stiff, she didn't know.

"It *is* an option. Donna already saw me reading those papers when she served us coffee at the diner."

"She saw you reading papers, period. She has no idea that they belonged to Lou Ann. So you *will* act surprised if they come up in conversation, and if you don't say yes, I won't let you take part in this interview."

That brought on a little outrage. "Excuse me?" She tried to move again, but he held her firmly in place.

"Just agree. If we keep this up, we'll both be so aroused we won't be able to walk. That's hardly the deportment necessary for conducting a crucial interview, now is it?"

That was like a mental slap back to reality. He was right. Damn him. Body contact with Sloan had a unique way of reminding her that she was a woman, but it did nothing to make her remember that she was a cop.

"Deal," she agreed through semiclenched teeth. Carley admired his attempts to keep her safe, she truly did, but there was a fine line between safety and not doing her job. She had no intentions of crossing that line.

Sloan and she took a minute, which turned to several minutes, so they could regain their composure and level their breathing.

"After this, we need to talk," Sloan informed her. "About sex."

Carley stared at him. "Sex," she repeated. "You think that's wise?"

"No. But avoiding it isn't working, either. So sex talk is on the agenda after we do this good cop/bad cop thing with Leland and Donna."

"We can talk all you want," Carley said. There was haughtiness in her voice, but it was pure facade. "But we're not having sex."

It seemed as if he changed his mind a dozen times as to what he wanted to say or do. But when he made his move, he moved.

He reached out, lightning-fast, and hooked his hand around her neck. Sloan hauled her to him and in the same motion he kissed her.

He took her mouth as if he owned her.

And Carley let him.

She stood there, dumbfounded and hotter than summer asphalt, while he used that clever mouth and tongue to remind her that she wanted him. Bad.

He broke the kiss only when they remembered that they needed air to live.

"That's why we have to talk," Sloan insisted, gulping in a huge breath. "This attraction is not going away just because it doesn't fit into our career plans."

"No. It doesn't fit," she agreed. "So what do we do about it? Other than the obvious," Carley added when she noticed that the look in his eyes was primitive and all male. The kind of look a man gave a woman before dragging her to the floor for some great sex.

Which suddenly sounded, well, *great.*

"How do we deal with this?" he asked. "We think of our respective badges. We think about how good it'll feel to toss Donna or Leland in jail."

Carley did think about it and she nodded. "It's working."

"Good. Keep at it. Jail. Key. Interview. Good cop. Bad cop. Don't forget the part about acting surprised if anything about Lou Ann's papers come up."

She repeated those words to herself as she followed Sloan out of the room and across the hall. One look at Leland and Donna and it wasn't hard to recall why they were there. Either one of them could be a killer, and that brought out every facet of Carley's obsession to serve them both a double dose of justice.

"Am I under arrest?" Leland barked.

Sloan shook his head. "Not at this exact moment. But it's still early. Give me a few hours."

"If I'm not under arrest, I'm not staying. I know my rights." He got up to leave.

"Fine," Sloan fired back. "I'm sure your ex-wife will be more than happy to speculate as to what you were doing last night."

That stopped Leland in his tracks. He slowly turned back around to face Sloan.

"And if you stay," Sloan continued, "then you

can return the favor. You can speculate as to what Donna was doing out and about until 3:00 a.m."

Carley could see the spark in Leland's eyes. He wouldn't pass up the chance to take a verbal shot at his ex.

"Donna doesn't have an alibi for last night?" Leland smugly asked.

"Nope," Sloan supplied. "But then, neither do you."

Some of Leland's obvious glee evaporated. "I went out for a drive. Last I heard, that wasn't a crime."

Carley decided it was time to play her part of the good cop. "No one is accusing you of anything, Leland. In fact, I think you know where I stand on the subject of who's guilty of these murders."

Leland looked at her with skepticism, as if she'd just showered him with thousands of dollar bills. "Then why haven't you put a leash on him?" Leland tipped his head toward Sloan.

"Because the Rangers have authority here," Donna commented. She gave her delicate pearl-and-coral earring an adjustment. "Isn't that right?"

"That's right." And Carley made sure she sounded riled and disgruntled. It wasn't difficult to do. She *was* disgruntled. "Sloan and I don't agree as to how to conduct this investigation. Nor do we have the same interpretation of the evidence. For instance, he believes it was you at the inn last night."

"Specifically I believe you were in the corridor that leads to the kitchen," Sloan added. "I think that's where you fired shots at us."

With that bit of misinformation, Carley studied both Leland's and Donna's expressions. She was certain Sloan was doing the same. However, if either of their suspects was surprised with that incorrect account of a kitchen vs. a hall shooting, neither showed it.

Frustrated, Carley pressed them. "I'm sure someone can verify where you were last night."

"No one," Donna quickly supplied.

That caused a sneer to form on Leland's mouth. "Probably because you were at the inn, shooting at them. She's good with a gun, you know. Her daddy made sure of that. Used to take her into the woods for target practice right before he sent her off to all those cotillion balls."

Donna examined her perfectly manicured finger-nails and centered a ring that had twisted around. "I have no reason to shoot them. I'm not the one who set up a fake kidnapping and murder. This sort of illegal activity is more your forte, Leland. And, for the record, you're a good shot, as well. If they need proof of that, all they have to do is look at the repaired wall in the family room where you shot holes in our wedding portrait."

Carley made sure she didn't smile at the verbal banter, but it was hard to hold back. This was exactly what Sloan and she wanted.

Sloan sat at the end of the small metal table and snared Donna's gaze. "You know, if the grand jury indicts Leland, you'll have to testify as to what you know about that fake kidnapping plan."

"Gladly."

"Well, maybe you won't do it so gladly when you have to testify as to where you got the money that you allegedly were going to use to pay off Lou Ann."

Donna looked as if he'd slapped her.

"Oh, I can help with that," Leland offered. That garnered him an icy stare from Donna. "She had a hidden offshore bank account. A huge one that she concealed from me so I wouldn't get my part during the divorce. Here I was fighting for my business, my home, the future of our children, and she hid what should be rightfully mine."

"It wasn't yours. It was *mine.*"

Leland made a yeah-right sound. "Money you planned to use to buy your liquor and pills." He turned his gaze toward Carley. "Donna likes the expensive stuff and lots of it."

If looks could kill, Donna would have murdered Leland with that icy glare. "I haven't had a drink or a pill in years. Once I was rid of you, I discovered I didn't need alcohol or pain medication to get through the day."

"Oh, so now it's my fault. Come on, Donna." Leland leaned closer to her and dropped his voice. "Admit it. Once a lush, always a lush."

She leaned in closer, too. "Come on, Leland. Admit it. Once a bastard, always a bastard." The pulse jumped in Donna's throat. "Because of you, our daughter Joey hasn't spoken to either of us in years, and I lost my son to God knows who or what. As far as I'm concerned, hell is too good a place for you, Leland Hendricks." Donna whipped around toward Sloan. "I'll gladly testify against him. In fact, the sooner the better."

Inside, Carley cheered. Sloan's plan to interview them together was working.

"Then how about we start now?" Sloan suggested. "Do you have any proof that Leland was anywhere near the inn last night?"

"No." Donna tucked a strand of her perfectly styled flame-red hair behind her ear. "But he's capable of murder. He's capable of anything."

"And you're not?" Leland fired back. "That inn is your home turf, Donna. Not mine. Besides, if I wanted someone dead, I wouldn't go prowling around in the dark."

"How did you know the gunman prowled in the dark?" Sloan fired back. Unlike Donna and Leland, there was no emotion in his voice.

The room went silent.

"The shooting happened at night," Leland said, his face strained. "It would have been dark. Hence the prowling comment."

Donna's pale ruby-colored mouth curved into a

smile. Leland obviously saw that smile and he had a reaction. Boy, did he. He hurled some vicious profanity at her, aimed a little more at Sloan and headed for the door. "This interview is over. If you want to talk to me again, call my lawyer."

With his exit, Donna stood. "That's advice I should take, as well." She spared each of them a glance. "And just let me know when you need me to testify against him." Tucking her trim leather purse beneath her arm, she strolled out the door.

Carley and Sloan waited until they heard the front door close before they looked at each other. They shared a smile.

"So is Leland guilty or was that a slip of the tongue?" Carley asked.

"It's hard to say." He blew out a long breath and propped his elbows on the table. "But I think we need to keep pressing them and, if possible, we need to do that while they're together. That volatility is something else, and it could be their undoing."

"Yes. But it's my guess we won't get either of them in here without their attorneys."

Sloan shrugged. "I don't think even their attorneys can hold them back when they're spewing venom at each other. We need to keep pressing," he repeated. His eyes met hers. "That's true with you, too. You need to keep going back to the night of Sarah's murder. What could you have possibly seen that would make a killer want you dead?"

"Nothing." Carley repeated it. "In fact, the only things I saw were legs and boots. After that, the next thing I recall in great detail is my face falling toward the dirt after I was shot."

He shook his head. "We're missing something. We have to be or the killer wouldn't be after you. If it's not something you saw the night of Sarah's murder, then maybe it was something sixteen years ago. Go back to the night Lou Ann was killed. Walk through everything that happened before the body was discovered."

Carley groaned. She didn't want to do this, but obviously Sloan thought it was necessary. "I've already told you that I saw you walking on Main Street that night." And since it seemed stupid to withhold it any longer, Carley finished the rest of the account. "I also followed you for a while."

Sloan stared at her. Shook his head. Stared some more. "Why?"

Carley toyed with the notion of stopping, but if she did, Sloan would just press her for the truth. No. It was time to spill the beans. "Because of Johnny Depp."

He pulled up a chair and had her sit, as well. "Please explain that."

There was no way to make this sound good or even semigood, so she just blurted out what'd happened. "I was reading that fan magazine and was, uh, thinking romantic thoughts."

"You were thinking romantic thoughts about *me?*"

"Sort of. In a transference kind of way." She paused, frowned. "Okay, now that I've told you that, I'll obviously have to move to another town, change my name and forever live with the embarrassment of just having admitted that I had the hots for you."

He didn't smile, but that damn twinkle in his eye made her think he was amused. "That's the night I discovered you had breasts. And a mouth."

That eased some of her embarrassment, but it did confuse her. "O-kay."

"I dream about your mouth."

"And what's my mouth doing in your dreams?" she asked cautiously but then held up her hand. "Wait, don't answer that."

Sloan nodded. "Excellent decision."

Yes. And it was obviously time to make another decision to drop this subject entirely. Why was it that every time Sloan and she got together the subject turned to either sex or murder? Probably because those were the only things they had in common.

Lust and the case.

Except Carley wasn't sure that was true. It was starting to feel like more. Much more. And that frightened her almost as much as not being able to identify a killer and stop that killer from striking again.

Sloan's cell phone rang, and while she was mulling over her sudden fear of feelings, he answered it.

"Zane," he greeted. He paused. "Let me click on the speaker so that Carley can hear this." He pressed a button and set his phone on the table.

"It's not good news, Carley," Zane continued a moment later. "We weren't able to recover any fingerprints from your apartment."

Even though she'd expected that, she felt the disappointment. A single fingerprint could have lead to an arrest. Still, they had other avenues. "How about gunpowder residue? Did it show up on one or both of our primary suspects?"

"Nothing there, either. If Donna or Leland fired those shots last night, they were wearing gloves," Zane concluded. "The crime lab also looked at both surveillance videos—the one from the police station and the other from Mildred Kerrville's shop. Nothing definitive, but we've decided to check rental-car places since that dark-colored sedan wasn't local. We might get lucky. In the meantime, I want you two to figure out why this shooter keeps coming after Carley."

"Carley and I were just going through this. Other than what she's already told us, she doesn't remember seeing anything the nights Sarah or Lou Ann were killed."

Carley looked at him, mumbled a thanks.

"It'll cost you," Sloan mouthed, nearly smiling.

She was afraid of that. She owed him a favor now. Not that he'd pressed her to do something for him.

No, that wasn't it. But with each near smile, each secret shared—heck, with every conversation—they were getting closer. Carley could feel it and yet was totally incapable of stopping it.

The empathetic look Sloan gave her let her know that he felt the same way.

They were *so* in trouble here.

"Then maybe this is just a simple case of the murderer doing overkill," Zane continued. "Carley is the only person who got close to Sarah's murderer that night, and since it's probably someone Carley knows…" Zane let that trail off. "Carley, perhaps you'd be willing to talk with the Rangers' psychiatrist?"

Since she was still thinking about Sloan and the trouble they were in, it took a moment for Carley to grasp what Zane had said. "You think I'm crazy?" she asked.

"No. But this shrink has been trained to uncover details in eyewitnesses' accounts and testimony. At least consider it, for the sake of the case."

Until he'd added that last part, Carley was about to answer with an unequivocal no to someone picking apart her account or her brain, but she couldn't say no to that. She had to do whatever it took to catch this killer.

"All right," Carley said. "I'll do it. But there's another person who might have witnessed Lou Ann's murder. Your father. He was there at the inn that night, I'm positive of that, and he might have seen something he hasn't remembered."

Because she was still facing Sloan, Carley had no trouble seeing his reaction. It wasn't as negative as she figured it would be. He actually seemed to be considering it. Which couldn't have been an easy thing, especially since his father might have killed Lou Ann—even if he didn't remember doing it.

"Okay," Zane concurred. "I'll call Dad and see if he'll try this approach. I'll let you know what he says."

Carley wouldn't hold her breath that Jim McKinney would agree. Potentially he was a man with a lot to hide.

"Sloan, you told Carley about the new sleeping arrangements?" Zane asked.

Sloan broke eye contact with her. "Not yet. I'll do it now. 'Bye, Zane."

"What sleeping arrangements?" she asked as he clicked the end-call button.

Sloan cleared his throat. "From now on, you'll be rooming with me."

Because his explanation didn't sound either serious or *sane,* Carley mentally repeated it word for word. She still didn't get it. "Excuse me?"

"You heard me, and it's not up for negotiation." He got to his feet and stared down at her. "You're moving in with me. If I could, I'd hide you away in a safe house, but since you're the sheriff and part of this investigation, that wouldn't be practical."

She shook her head and stated the obvious. "There's no way we can be roommates."

"Oh, yes, there is. I need someone to watch my back, and you need someone to watch yours. Think about it, Carley. This person wants overkill, and that means I'm now a target since I saw the shooter last night."

Oh, God.

He was right. Sloan was now in danger from the same SOB who wanted her dead.

Carley's stomach sank. Her breath vanished. Why hadn't she thought of this sooner? Sloan was just as much at risk as she was.

"We don't have a choice," Sloan added.

No. They apparently didn't. But that didn't make this any easier to accept. Because daylight didn't last forever. Nightfall would come a lot sooner than she wanted. And that meant Sloan and she would be alone.

In the same room.

Together.

Chapter Twelve

"Have I mentioned that this really isn't a good idea?" Carley called out from the bathroom.

"Yeah. You've mentioned it," Sloan answered. And though he wasn't counting, Sloan figured that she'd mentioned it at least a dozen times. She would no doubt mention it a dozen more before the night was over.

Why?

Because despite their inability to keep their hands and mouths off each other, they were going to sleep in the same room.

Well, he hoped *sleep* was all they'd do tonight. They both needed some rest and they definitely didn't need any other activity.

Especially sex.

The bathroom door opened and Carley stepped out. Fully clothed, thank goodness. In fact, she wore mint-green pajamas and a matching ankle-length robe. There was nothing remotely sexy about the outfit, but Sloan couldn't say the same about the woman wearing it.

Carley had taken off what little makeup she'd previously had on, and her hair lay loose and mussed on her shoulders. The lack of adornment allowed him to concentrate on just how beautiful she was.

Oh, man.

Sloan shook his head. Best not to think of her great looks tonight. Instead he turned back to Lou Ann's notes that he should be studying.

"I'll bet you sleep naked," Carley mumbled under her breath.

So much for studying. Sloan almost laughed. "Normally I do. But, trust me, I'll be fully clothed tonight." In fact, maybe he'd wear his holster and boots. Spurs, even. It'd be a surefire way to keep him from removing his pants.

"Me, too. If I owned panty hose, I'd put them on beneath these PJs. Something tells me we're going to need all the chastity-belt type of help we can get."

Sloan nodded. "It'll also help if we keep some space between us. You take the bed. I'll take the floor."

She glanced at the hardwood floor. "I could have the desk clerk bring up a cot."

"I don't want anyone, including the clerk, to know which room we're staying in."

That was the reason he'd used Carley's master key to turn on the lights in some of the unoccupied rooms. It would make it difficult for the cloaked shooter to make a return visit if it wasn't common knowledge where Carley and he were specifically staying.

"I could go get a roll-away bed from the supply closet," she suggested.

He shook his head, vetoing that, as well. "And you'd risk someone seeing and following you. I don't want to take any chances."

"Yet here we are *together,* mere feet apart from each other. Don't say it," she quickly added. "It's an unavoidable risk. I know. But…"

There was no need for her to finish that statement. Sloan knew what she was thinking. Sleeping so close to each other could turn out to be the ultimate risk.

She grabbed extra blankets and bed linen from the top of the closet and deposited them onto the floor. They landed with a *kerplunk,* and Sloan could already feel the backache he'd have tomorrow. Still, a backache was a small price to pay for keeping Carley safe.

"Find anything new in Lou Ann's notes?" Carley asked.

"Not yet."

Carley threw back the covers on the bed and practically jumped in. She pulled the comforter all the way up to her chin. For long, quiet moments she said nothing, but Sloan could almost hear her thinking. It was either one of two things on her mind: the murder investigation or this insanity happening between them.

"I keep thinking about our confessions," Carley said softly. "About how we were attracted to each other all those years ago."

He groaned softly. Of the two possible subjects, this was the one he didn't want to discuss. Best to dismiss it. It was also best to delay that sex talk he'd promised her earlier. A conversation like that shouldn't happen when they were alone. In the same room.

With the air steaming between them.

"We were teenagers," he stated. "Attraction at that age isn't just common, it's a given."

"I guess. Are we going to have the sex talk now?" Carley asked.

Sloan nearly choked on his own breath. "I thought you'd forgotten about that."

"You're joking, right? After that kiss at the police station, you thought I'd forget that you wanted to discuss sex? Well, I didn't. So, talk. After all, it was your idea."

Yes. And in hindsight, it was a very bad one. An idea that'd formed in his head when he'd done the bump-and-grind session with Carley against the door. It'd been a way to defuse a situation.

It had worked. Temporarily. Sort of.

Now he'd need something to defuse the defusion tactic.

"Okay, I'll start," Carley volunteered. "We've acknowledged the attraction. We've acted on it a little. But we can't act on it further without jeopardizing our careers."

Man, he wished that were true and he knew this for a fact because he'd given it too much thought. "At worst, acting on it would just cause us to lose focus. And at best, it would be very, very good."

She laughed. It was throaty, filled with nerves and excitement. Because this conversation was definitely taboo. "I like you, Sloan. I mean, I really like you, and that's more frightening to me than the sexual attraction."

Sloan agreed, but it was best not to voice it. They'd already crossed too many lines tonight.

"We should probably get some rest," he reminded her. Sloan got up from the table and, without bothering to remove any items of clothing, he crawled onto his makeshift bed on the floor.

His preparations for sleep didn't put a cap on the conversation.

"This has been going on for a long time," she continued. "On my part, anyway. That night when I realized you were a fairly hot guy, I considered the possibilities. I mean, we both knew we wanted to be cops, even then. And my teenage brain began to weave a fantasy. Both of us serving as deputies, side by side. Then maybe one day cosheriffs."

"Cosheriffs? Not in Justice. The city has enough trouble paying one."

"It was a fantasy," she grumbled, sounding as if he'd just burst her bubble. "And I'm rambling. Sorry, I do that when I'm nervous."

"Yeah. I understand."

He wasn't nervous but anxious. Anxious about their sleeping arrangements. Anxious about the case. Anxious about the silence. Because with the silence gave his body too much time to come up with other ideas.

Bad ideas.

"That cosheriff fantasy was a good one," he commented. He gave it some thought. "And it all came crashing down the night of Lou Ann's murder."

She sat up, stuffed some pillows behind her back and peered down at him. Since they'd intentionally left the overhead light on, he had no trouble seeing her. "It stung when you didn't believe that I'd seen your father coming out of Lou Ann's room that night."

"I'm sorry," Sloan said because it was a long overdue apology.

Carley didn't exactly accept that apology, but she did continue. "In addition to lusting after you, I idolized you. You had it all. Great grades, athletic ability, popularity."

"I also had a totally dysfunctional family," he reminded her. "It was that year that I learned my father had an illegitimate son and had seemingly slept with every adult female in town. Coupled with

Lou Ann's murder, it nearly destroyed my parents' marriage. Which wouldn't have necessarily been such a bad thing," he added.

Carley kept her attention solely on him. "Why exactly did your mother stay with your dad after she learned of his affairs and his other son?"

"The truth? Sometimes I think it's so she can punish him. This way, she can remind him on a daily basis of how much he hurt her."

"He hurt all of you," Carley pointed out.

"True. That includes you. He hurt you by default by placing himself in a situation where he should have never been."

She shrugged. "Life's like that sometimes. We were all just breezing along before that night. Lou Ann's murder stopped the breezing and made us take a cold, hard look at ourselves."

"And it tore this town apart," Sloan concluded. "That's why we need to find her killer. We need to end this so the entire town can heal."

The silence settled uncomfortably between them and it made Sloan wonder if she disagreed with his comment. Maybe the town wouldn't heal. Maybe he wouldn't heal if he learned that his father was involved.

No, not involved.

Guilty.

Just thinking about it caused his stomach to churn. But he wasn't a naive sixteen-year-old kid anymore. He had to accept the possibility that his father had done the unthinkable.

Or, if not his father, someone else close to him.

"I've been keeping something from you," he heard himself say.

Carley frowned. "This isn't more of that sex talk, is it?"

"No. I almost wish that it were. It'd be easier than what I have to tell you. It's about something that happened the night Lou Ann was murdered sixteen years ago."

Her frown deepened.

"Over the years I've tried to convince myself that it wasn't important," he continued. "But the truth is I just don't know anymore."

"This is about your father?"

"Not exactly." Sloan tucked his hands behind his head. "I went looking for my father that night. I even walked around the inn to see if I could find him with Lou Ann. I didn't. All the curtains were closed in the rooms on the bottom floor. I didn't want to come inside to look because you were there—and you would have asked questions."

"So you left. That must have been when I spotted you and followed you?"

"Probably. Though I really didn't notice you following me. I just kept thinking that I needed to find Dad. I needed to convince him to stop seeing Lou Ann."

"But you didn't find him," Carley concluded.

"No. I went back to my house. No one was there."

He waited and watched his words register on Carley's face. "Zane was at college," she said as if thinking out loud. "So where was your mother?"

"I don't know. I called out her name and she didn't answer. The following morning I asked her about it, and she said she was asleep, that she'd taken her migraine meds and they'd knocked her out."

"Did you believe her?"

"At the time. Because I *wanted* to believe her. But the light was on in her bedroom. If she'd had a migraine, she would have turned off the lights."

"Wow," Carley mumbled. A moment later she repeated it. "Why didn't you tell this to the sheriff sixteen years ago?"

"You probably won't believe this, but I forgot all about it until Sarah's death. I didn't repress it, but I was totally sidetracked by my father's arrest. The sheriff didn't really even investigate the murder. He certainly didn't ask if my mother had an alibi. Right from the start, he was convinced that my father was guilty."

"So was I."

Sloan looked up at her. He'd expected to see some condemnation or at least a little anger that he hadn't told her this before, but there was only sympathy.

"The gender bias was at work back then," Carley explained. She climbed out of bed and eased down onto the floor, sitting beside him. "Sheriff Wainwright was in charge then and he was as old-school as they come. He probably took one look at your mom—feminine, pale, vulnerable, president of the Garden Club—and he probably didn't believe that Stella McKinney was capable of swatting a fly, much less strangling a woman."

Yeah. That'd no doubt been the old sheriff's thinking. "Still, I should have told someone."

She reached out and skimmed her finger along his cheek. Not in a sexual way. She was obviously trying to comfort him. "It wouldn't have done any good. No one, including me, would have listened." Carley paused. "But I'm listening now and I still can't see your mother—all ninety-five pounds of her—going after a wildcat like Lou Ann."

Sloan played around that image, and while it seemed unlikely, it wasn't impossible. Adrenaline and anger were huge factors in a physical confrontation, and despite his mother's delicate size, he'd seen her angry enough to do just about anything.

Carley plucked his cell phone from his holster. "But you should tell Zane. Just for the record. Just so it doesn't come back later to bite you in the butt."

Sloan nodded, wishing he'd done it ages ago. Or at least at the onset of the most recent murder investigation.

Dreading the conversation, Sloan pressed in his brother's number. "Zane—" he said when his brother answered.

"Sloan, I was about to call you. I just had a very interesting conversation with our father."

That put a halt to the confession Sloan was about to make. "What did he want?"

"He said he's willing to see the Rangers' psychiatrist, and he wants us to set it up."

That was the last thing he'd expected from his father, and Sloan's own reaction was mixed. "What made him agree to it?"

"He said he needs to get to the truth."

"After sixteen years?" Sloan thought *Why now?* but didn't voice it to his brother. "So when is this session going to happen?"

"Day after tomorrow. Cross your fingers, Sloan. We might finally learn what happened the night that Lou Ann was murdered."

"Yes," Sloan mumbled.

"Why did you call?" Zane asked. "Something to do with the case?"

"Maybe." Now how to put this? It wasn't easy to say, especially with the news about his father spinning through his head. "Mom might not have been home the night Lou Ann was killed."

Zane paused. "What do you mean?"

Sloan suddenly felt foolish, but then Carley began to rub his arm, and it had a surprisingly soothing effect. "I mean I can't say with certainty that she was there."

"Are you trying to tell me she's a suspect?"

Sloan scrubbed his hand over his face. "I don't know what I'm saying. I just wanted you to know."

"And now I know," Zane said. Not in a matter-of-fact tone. There was emotion. Lots of it. Old wounds that just wouldn't heal. "Reinterview her in a day or two. Better yet, have Carley do it. Have Carley press her hard. If Mom is hiding something, I want to know what."

That was the big question—was his mother hiding something? If so, what? Had she gone to the inn and seen Lou Ann? Or better yet, had Stella seen her own husband with another woman?

"My dad agreed to see the shrink," Sloan relayed to Carley once he'd hung up the phone.

"That's gutsy of him."

Gutsy or maybe even stupid. He wasn't sure which.

Sloan only hoped he could live with the *truth* that his father—and mother—might give them.

Chapter Thirteen

As if it were a rattler coiled and ready to strike, Carley picked up the letter that the deputy had deposited on her temporary desk the next morning. She hadn't thought she had any adrenaline left in her body, but she'd obviously been wrong.

She felt the adrenaline roar through her. She also felt the trepidation and the queasy feeling that went right along with it.

Sloan must have noticed the change in her body language, because he got up from his own temporary desk and went to her. "Something wrong?"

"No." And before he could get a glimpse of the return address on the envelope, Carley shoved the letter into the center drawer. It was apparently like waving a red flag in front of a charging bull.

"You might as well tell me what that was," he warned, "or I'll just keep bugging you."

"No, you won't. You'll get back to work reading Sarah's notes and setting up that interview with your mother. We need a break in this case so things can get back to normal. This place is making me claustrophobic."

She made a sweeping glance around the tiny room that they were now sharing as an office. There were no windows. Not anymore. Several years earlier the space had been modified from an office to do double duty as an extra jail cell and interrogation room. It felt more like the former than the latter. But, of course, without windows, the gunman wouldn't have an easy way to make a repeat attack.

"A diversionary tactic," Sloan commented. "Nice try. But it won't work. When you saw that letter, you looked as if you were facing a life-or-death situation."

Well, it wasn't that grave. But it was close.

Carley stared at him, waiting for him to return to his desk. He didn't. She didn't know why she thought he would. Sloan wasn't going to drop this.

"If you must know, it's a letter from the Rangers' selection board. I suspect it'll let me know if I've made it to the next round of the selection process." She moistened her lips. "Or if my application has been declined."

Sloan's expression brightened. "Then open it and find out which."

"Later." She tried to sound nonchalant and was sure she failed.

Carley took a deep breath, ready to defend her

decision, but a defense wasn't necessary. She was saved by the bell. Or, rather, the ringing from Sloan's cell phone. He tossed her a look that let her know this conversation wasn't over and he took the call.

Sloan, too, went through a change in body language after just a few seconds. He became focused on the call. Carley listened to his responses to try to figure out what was going on. Judging from his clipped voice, this was something big and it was connected to the case.

"What happened?" she demanded the moment he hung up the phone.

"That call was from a fellow Ranger who's been tailing Donna all morning. He followed her into Dallas, where she went into a bank and bought a cashier's check for a thousand dollars. The Ranger questioned the clerk and the bank manager. They finally admitted that Donna buys a thousand-dollar cashier's check every month."

"A thousand dollars," Carley repeated. And in the form of a cashier's check, at that. "So who's the recipient?"

Sloan shook his head. "The bank employees didn't know. Do you think this could be blackmail money?"

"Possibly. But who would be blackmailing her?"

"Leland, maybe?"

Carley made a sound of disagreement. "She'd rather eat razor blades than give money to her ex."

"Maybe he didn't give her a choice."

"Yes. That would be the only way Donna would pay him. But Leland's not the only possibility. Basically it could be anyone who might have seen Donna near Lou Ann that night. Maybe Donna's paying hush money to keep her presence unknown because just being in the vicinity of Lou Ann's murder would be enough for us to arrest her."

"True. If it is blackmail money."

"You have another idea?" Carley asked.

"Too many of them. Maybe she has a gambling habit. Or a pet charity project. Maybe she's making payments to someone who loaned her money off the books. It could even be some kind of investment scheme that's perfectly legal—"

"Okay. I see what you mean. The monthly checks could be sinister. Or not." Carley snapped her fingers. "Where did Donna go *after* she left the bank?"

Sloan couldn't stop himself from frowning. "While the Ranger was talking with the bank manager, he requested that a plainclothes officer from Dallas PD follow Donna. The officer lost her."

Until Sloan added that last part, Carley's hopes were soaring. That caused them to sink like deadweight. "He did what?"

"There was a traffic jam, and he ended up several cars behind her. Donna caught the traffic light just right and sped off. He couldn't catch up with her."

"Well, that's just great. We'll have to wait another month before she buys another check. And it might not even happen. She might have noticed the cop following her. If she's suspicious, it could be the last time she steps foot in that bank."

"Yeah. I considered that. But if Donna got suspicious, it means she has something to hide."

"The question is, what?"

"There's only one way to find out. We put her back under surveillance until she gives us what we need to know." Sloan took out his phone. "And I'll see if any businesses or office buildings around that traffic jam in Dallas had exterior surveillance cameras."

"Great idea. Because if she gave that check to someone in Dallas, we might have video proof of it."

"And it might break this case wide-open," Sloan concurred.

That got Carley to work. She grabbed the number for the Dallas police so she could start making calls. Maybe it wouldn't take long to contact the businesses who might have recorded Donna's car and ultimately her destination.

Then Carley could find a quiet place, away from Sloan, to read the letter. No matter the results, it would change her life forever.

"ANY LUCK?" SLOAN ASKED.

Carley shook her head. "You?"

"Not yet." It was an overly optimistic answer considering he had no more calls on his list to make. So far, he'd phoned sixteen places of business and requested that they review their surveillance systems to see if they'd captured the image of Donna's car in that Dallas traffic jam.

Not one had.

"How many more places do you have left to call?" Sloan asked Carley.

She made a zero with her index finger and thumb. "Shop owners apparently don't make a habit of aiming their cameras at traffic."

"So it seems. Still, I have a jewelry store owner who says he'll call back when he closes up for the night." Sloan checked his watch. It was six-thirty. "Which should have already happened."

"Maybe he'll call tomorrow." But she didn't sound any more convinced of that than Sloan was.

She stood, stretched and winced a little.

"You need your pain meds?" Sloan asked.

"No way. I plan to work late tonight going over Sarah's notes. Besides, my side's not really hurting. Just a twinge every now and then."

Because he wanted to look into her eyes to see if that was true, he stood, as well, and went to her desk. He leaned in, violating her personal space. She didn't exactly back away, but she did give him a be-careful stare.

Sloan smiled.

So did Carley.

But the jingling of the bell on the door wiped the smiles from both their faces.

Because it was past normal duty hours and because of the recent attempts to kill them, Sloan drew his weapon. He didn't put it away either when he heard the clicks of the person's footsteps.

Delicate steps.

Which meant their visitor was a woman. He aimed his gun anyway. After all, one of their main suspects was a woman.

However, this wasn't Donna Hendricks, but it was a woman he didn't want to have to face tonight.

His mother.

Stella stopped in the doorway of the interrogation room/temporary office. As always, she was dressed to perfection in a turquoise-colored dress and white heels. There wasn't a strand of dark hair out of place, and she wore only the lightest of makeup.

"We need to talk," Stella greeted, snaring Sloan's gaze. Her voice was feathery-soft. Like the woman herself. His mother definitely had a waiflike appearance.

Carley must have taken his mother's statement as her cue to leave because she started for the door. Stella blocked her exit. "Stay. You're part of this."

Carley nodded and returned to her seat. "What can I do for you, Mrs. McKinney?"

"You can listen." Stella remained in the doorway

and she clutched her small white purse in front of her as if it were a shield. "Jim told me about Zane setting up the session with the psychiatrist. I'm going to speak frankly. Zane doesn't care about his father and he certainly doesn't have Jim's best interest at heart." She turned toward Sloan. "But I thought you would. I thought I could count on you to protect him."

"Are you saying it's not in Dad's best interest to attend that session?" Sloan asked.

"You know it's not."

Sloan was still straddling the fence on that one, but he had to concede, privately, that his mother might be right. "It was Dad's decision to do this."

"Hardly." His mother extracted a crisp white linen handkerchief from her purse and pressed it to her cheek. "Zane talked him into doing it. Jim would do anything to get back in Zane's good graces and he thinks this is the way to go about it. On the other hand, Zane would do anything to clear this case because every day that it goes unsolved is a black mark on his precious career."

"I don't know Zane's motives regarding his father," Carley spoke up. "But if your husband is innocent, what harm would it do for him to see the shrink?"

"What harm?" Stella pulled in a weak but ragged breath. "With the exception of Sloan, this entire town has wanted to see Jim behind bars. They don't even care if he's innocent. They just want someone, *anyone,* to pay for those murders so they'll feel safer at night."

"Mom, Zane and I are only after the truth," Sloan insisted.

"The three of you are lawmen above all else." Stella blotted harder with her handkerchief. "Your father is easily swayed, and I have no doubt that a psychiatrist could trick him into confessing."

Sloan shook his head. "That wouldn't happen."

"I don't believe you." She neatly placed her handkerchief back into her purse and then snapped it shut. "Your father has been through enough. *I've* been through enough. Judging from what everyone is saying, you have your suspects—Leland and Donna. That's all you need. And I'm begging you to leave your father alone."

Sloan wasn't immune to the thick tears that sprang to his mother's eyes, but he also knew that she was capable of using those tears to get what she wanted. "Shouldn't Dad have a say in this?"

"No."

That was it. One of Stella's decrees. She would have probably left then and there if Sloan hadn't stopped her. As unpleasant as this conversation was, he had to extend it a little longer.

God help him.

Stella likely wouldn't kill the messenger, but she wouldn't let him off scot-free either.

"Mom, I have two things I need to tell you. One, Carley is going to have to reinterview you about the night Lou Ann was killed."

Stella spared Carley a glance. "Call me. We'll set up a time." What his mother didn't do was ask why, after all these years, she would need to be questioned again. "You said there were two things," she prompted Sloan.

Yes, and while she'd taken the first one quite well, Sloan wasn't counting on the second going down that way. "You need to know that in a few days Cole will be coming to town."

Stella stared at him with accusing eyes. "I see."

"We need Cole on the case," Sloan explained. Though Sloan didn't clarify that, as a tracker, Cole would be going through the woods and looking for evidence. Best not to spread that news around.

Stella shook her head. "Bringing that man here wasn't a very bright idea." She didn't wait for him to answer. "You know what'll happen, don't you? If he's here, it'll be like rubbing your father's indiscretions in my face."

"I'm sorry you feel that way, but Cole is being brought in because he's very good at what he does."

Stella made a sharp sound to indicate she didn't believe that. "This tells me exactly how much regard you have for my feelings and for me. Obviously you have no regard at all. Well, two can play that game. If you want to see your father, then you'll do so only with his attorney present. The same goes for you, Carley. I won't let Jim be railroaded into anything, whether it's by the sheriff or his own sons. It ends *here*. It ends *now*."

His mother turned as if to leave, but then she stopped and looked at Sloan again. "If you love your father as much as you say you do, you'll stay away from him."

There was no melodrama in her tone. No hot emotion. Stella's order was glacier-cold. As was the parting glance she aimed at both of them.

"You think you can convince your father to do the session?" Carley asked. "Or is Stella's word gospel?"

"Gospel," Sloan assured her. He walked up the hall and locked the door, something he wished he'd done a lot sooner. He also turned off the front lights to deter any other visitors. "My father won't challenge her, trust me."

Carley stepped out into the hall and stared at him, apparently waiting for him to elaborate. He didn't. There was no sense telling her that his father was often spineless when it came to Stella.

"Jim lets her punish him because he feels he deserves it," Carley muttered.

And that was the truth. Well, in one way. "Guilty of the affairs, the cheating?"

"Yes. That's what I meant. I wasn't trying to pick a fight about your father's involvement or lack thereof with the murders." She glanced down at her notes. "Truth is, everything seems to be pointing to Donna."

He was relieved. And thankful that Carley hadn't pushed the other reason that his father might feel guilty. "Now if we could just find some solid evidence to tie her to these crimes. The D.A.'s going to need that if the grand jury decides there's enough to have Donna arrested."

Carley nodded. "So we keep digging through Lou Ann's notes and we have the Ranger continue to follow Donna."

In some ways that seemed futile, but it was the only course of action they had.

Sloan checked his watch. "It's late. How about we call it a night…after you read your letter, of course."

Carley blinked as if she'd forgotten all about it. Sloan seriously doubted that she had. That letter was too important to her future.

"I can step into the hall while you read it," he suggested. "If you want some privacy."

Her silence let him know she was considering it, but then she shook her head and extracted the letter from the desk drawer.

"Here goes nothing," Carley mumbled, tearing it open. She unfolded the single sheet of paper and silently began to read.

Sloan didn't realize he was holding his breath until he felt his lungs start to ache. He also hadn't realized just how much he had vested in this, emotionally. But he apparently had a lot. He suddenly wished that he hadn't pressed Carley to open the letter. Because if this was bad news, then delaying it might have been a good thing.

Or not.

Heck. He didn't know if it was good or bad. He just knew he didn't have a clue what to say if—

"I made the second round cut," she said. Carley blew out a long breath. "My application was sent to the final board. I should know something within the next two days."

Sloan couldn't help it. He whooped for joy, and it was loud. A lot louder than Carley's laugh. He hurried to her, ready to scoop her into his arms and give her a Texas-size bear hug, but then he thought of her injury. He settled for something much gentler.

He pulled her to him.

"Oh, no," Carley whispered. "Celebratory happiness mixed with lust. A dangerous combination." She backed away from him. "With all this energy, even a simple kiss could land us in bed."

The thought of it slid through him.

Sloan forced himself to remember why that wasn't a good idea. It took a while, long moments in which he weighed the consequences. And he was finally able to see the wisdom of keeping some distance between them. He was ready to confirm it verbally.

But the sound stopped him.

It stopped Carley, too.

Both turned in the direction of the sound, which was apparently coming from the back door. Sloan had remembered to lock it earlier, mainly because it wasn't an entrance that should be used this time of night.

Even though someone was now testing the doorknob.

"Do you think your mother came back?" Carley whispered.

"No." In fact, Sloan had another theory, one that had him drawing his gun. "When I turned off the front lights, someone may have thought we'd left."

"So this is a break-in," she muttered, taking out her gun, as well.

With his heart pounding, Sloan braced himself for whatever was about to happen. But he hadn't braced himself for the phone to ring.

The sound shot through the room.

Carley gasped, probably because of the unexpected noise. They hadn't switched the phone to dispatch yet, even though it was well past normal duty hours.

But the caller perhaps wouldn't know that.

The person might be checking to see if Carley and he were still there.

Sloan waited for three rings, so that the intruder would think the call had been picked up by the dispatch service, and he lifted the phone from its cradle. He didn't say anything. He simply waited.

He didn't have to wait long.

'"Someone shot at me," a man shouted from the other end of the line.

It took Sloan a moment to realize that the caller was none other than Leland Hendricks. Sloan didn't have to ask the man what was happening because Leland continued on his own.

"I'm on the ground in the parking lot at the back of the inn. I'm hiding behind Carley's car and I don't have my gun with me. I swear, someone took a shot at me!"

Hell. What else could possibly go wrong tonight?

The doorknob continued to rattle, and Sloan could hear someone trying almost desperately to pick the lock.

"Do your job," Leland yelled. "Come and find the bastard who tried to kill me."

"Call for the deputies," Sloan relayed to Carley. "Have them go to the back of the inn. Someone just tried to kill Leland."

Carley cursed, too, but she made the call. Sloan estimated that it would take five to ten minutes for the deputies to arrive. That should be plenty of time for this to come to a head. After all, the person who'd shot at Leland—if there was indeed a shot—was likely now trying to break in. Leland would probably be safe from another attack.

Leland's frantic shouts, however, said otherwise.

"The SOB's trying to kill me," Leland yelled. "Get out here now."

Sloan might have played that down a little if the break-in continued. But it didn't. Suddenly there were no more sounds coming from the back door. In fact, the only sounds were Leland's shouts for help.

"I have to go out there," Sloan said to Carley. "You stay put."

"Not on your life. You can't go out there without backup."

"This person is gunning for you," Sloan reminded her.

"Apparently he or she is gunning for Leland right now. No matter what we think of him, I have a job to do. I can't just let him die."

Her voice was ripe with emotion, but beneath it he could hear the cop. Sloan could feel the cop in him, as well, and he knew he couldn't let an unarmed man be murdered.

Keeping his body against the wall, Sloan moved toward the front door. Not the back. There were too many places out there for a gunman to hide. Carley was right behind him.

Sloan unlocked the door and opened it. The hot, muggy air engulfed him. So did the doubts.

This could all be a setup.

If Leland was the killer, he could be using this call to draw them out into the open. That's the reason

Sloan forced Carley to stay behind him. It didn't please her, but he didn't care.

With his gun drawn and ready, Sloan stepped outside. He saw no one, but he could still hear Leland shouting for help.

"This way," Sloan told Carley.

Again he didn't lead her toward the back, but instead they kept to the sidewalk on Main Street. He slowed when he got to the narrow alley just before the inn and he peered around the corner to see if he could spot Leland.

He did.

The man was indeed cowering next to Carley's car. He didn't appear to be armed, but Sloan knew that appearances could be deceiving—and deadly.

"Are you all right?" Sloan called out to Leland.

Leland scurried to the back of the car, where he was out of Sloan's line of sight. A split second later there was that damn swishing sound again.

Sloan felt the bullet slice across his shoulder.

It was fiery-hot and it cut right through his flesh. He ignored the pain—or, rather, tried to as he ducked back behind the cover of the front of the building. Sloan cursed. Had Leland fired that shot? He couldn't tell.

"You're hurt," Carley said, her voice mostly breath.

Sloan didn't have time to let her know that he was okay. He didn't have time to do anything.

Because there was another shot fired.

And another.

The bullets slammed into the sidewalk, tearing out a chunk of concrete and coming so close to Carley that Sloan saw his life flash before his eyes.

Damn it, the shooter had moved. The person was probably in the woods. Or behind Carley's car. In other words, Sloan didn't know if the shots were coming from Leland or from someone in the woods just behind him.

Because this had to stop, because Carley could be killed, Sloan had to take drastic action. It was a risk. A huge one. But he had no choice.

"Let's go," he warned Carley.

But he didn't give her time to react. Sloan aimed toward the woods and fired. A diversion of sorts. So he could buy Carley and him some time.

He fired again. And again while he latched onto her with his left hand and hauled her toward the front of the inn.

Sloan plowed through the entrance, both Carley and he landing on the floor.

"Get down and call my brother," Sloan shouted to the desk clerk.

In the same breath, he pulled Carley into the corner. So they'd have cover. He wanted to comfort her, to assure her that all would be well.

But he couldn't.

He couldn't assure her of anything. Hell, he

couldn't even guarantee that he could keep her safe. But he could do everything within his power to catch this killer.

Or die trying.

Chapter Fourteen

Carley studied the McKinney brothers, Zane and Sloan. They were huddled in the corner of her living room, having a whispered but very intense conversation. She knew the intensity was sky-high because Sloan's jaw muscles were iron-stiff and his hands were white-knuckled. Every other word was one of harsh profanity.

"I'm not going to let you interrogate them," Zane insisted, his voice not quite a whisper for that comment. "Not while you're in this state of mind."

By *them*, Zane no doubt meant Donna and Leland. The state-of-mind reference was obvious, too. Sloan appeared to be on the verge of launching himself at anyone, including Zane, who would stand in the way of going after the person who'd tried to kill them tonight.

Sloan obviously didn't approve of Zane's directive. He stood there, glaring at his older brother. Cursing. Mumbling. Getting even more tense with each passing second. And this while Sloan still wore his blood-spattered shirt.

His own blood.

From the gunman's bullet slashing across his left shoulder blade.

The injury had been treated and stitched and was covered with a crisp white bandage. It was a minor injury, the medic had declared. Maybe physically it was. But for her, mentally, there was nothing minor about a bullet that'd come within a fraction of an inch of killing Sloan.

"Besides," Zane added, glancing at her. "You have to stay here with Carley. The gunman is still out there, and I don't want her left alone. At least not until we've had time to process the area for evidence."

She almost protested, because it made her sound weak. But the truth was, she didn't want Sloan back out there in the town tonight. Not after they'd come so close to being killed. Until her adrenaline had leveled, until her heartbeat had returned to at least seminormal, she didn't want him putting his life back on the line.

And if Sloan left the apartment, his life would definitely be on the line.

If she could keep Sloan safe under the guise of keeping her safe, it was worth any damage this would do to her image as sheriff.

"*Image,*" she mumbled under her breath. Suddenly that didn't mean a whole lot to her. But she knew what did: Sloan and solving this case.

But especially Sloan.

She'd come very close to losing him, and it might take her a couple of lifetimes to come to terms with the sickening feeling she had because of that.

Zane and Sloan finished their conversation. Well, sort of. Sloan cursed, threw his hands up in the air and stormed into the bathroom. He ripped off his bloody shirt along the way and hurled it at the trash can.

"He blames himself for this attack," Zane said to her.

Carley strolled toward him. "I understand. I blame myself, too. And neither of us likes to share that blame."

The corner of Zane's mouth lifted, but the smile didn't quite make it to his eyes. He cocked his head to the side, studying her. "I hadn't seen it before tonight. But I see it now."

Since that seemed like some kind of announcement of a personal relationship between Sloan and her, Carley didn't comment.

"It's not a bad thing, you know," Zane continued.

It could be, but she kept that to herself, as well.

"All right. Here's how this has to work," Zane continued. His voice was all business now. "You two stay put until the area behind the inn is cleared and processed. There'll be a deputy posted at the end of the hall, but I don't want Sloan or you to open the door to anyone."

"And then what?" she asked.

"You wait until you hear otherwise," Zane confirmed. "I'll round up Donna and have both Leland and her tested for gunshot residue. We didn't find a gun on Leland, but he could have easily tossed it into the woods."

"Was Leland hurt in the shooting?" Sloan asked.

Zane shook his head. "Not a scratch. That doesn't mean he's the shooter, but it doesn't mean he's innocent, either. We'll have to search the woods in the morning in case he tossed a gun there. I have a team who'll go through Donna and Leland's houses and vehicles, so they can look for anything that might link them to this attack."

In other words, this wasn't going to move quickly.

"I want you to try to get some rest," Zane went on, his tone a little less businesslike. "I need you to be a hundred percent for tomorrow afternoon."

Surprised, she stared at him. "What's happening tomorrow afternoon?"

"You'll likely be called to testify before the grand jury. If not tomorrow, then the following day for sure."

Carley groaned. With everything else going on, she'd forgotten about that. "I won't be able to tell them who tried to kill Sloan and me."

"I know. We just need your account of what happened the night you were shot."

Strange. Carley hadn't thought it possible, but that night was no longer the worst of her life. Oh, no. Since then, she'd been through much worse with the two attempts to kill Sloan and her.

"I heard about you making it to the next round for Ranger selection," Zane said.

Carley wasn't surprised. Zane was an important, powerful man within the Rangers organization. "It's a long shot," she answered.

"It always is." Zane opened the door, started to leave but then turned back to her. "I don't know how deep your feelings go for Sloan. I'm hoping they're *deep*."

"Why?" she asked, not at all certain she wanted to have this conversation.

"Because he's going need you to get through this. He's the good guy, Carley. The one who stayed behind in Justice and tried to take care of things when our family fell apart. That's what Sloan does— he takes care of things. He makes things right. He'll see what happened today as a personal failure."

Yes. He would.

"I'll smooth things over with him," she promised Zane. Though Carley had no idea how she could keep a promise like that.

"Good," Zane said. "Lock the door behind me."

She did, and it occurred to her that she'd been doing that a lot lately. Except this time she was locking herself in with Sloan.

Sloan, who needed soothing.

Oh, mercy.

Carley held out her hand, saw the tremble. She apparently could use some soothing, as well. The adrenaline was still there. It created a nervous energy all its own and, coupled with the other things she was feeling, everything suddenly seemed out of control. And more than a little dangerous.

She wasn't thinking about the killer, either.

But about Sloan.

There was a surefire way to burn off some of this excess energy. That was the dangerous part. Because it involved human contact. With Sloan.

Carley did a mental check to make sure that was what she wanted.

It was.

No doubt about it. In fact, she didn't think she'd ever wanted anything more than this. So she took a deep breath and headed toward the bathroom.

Sloan had left the door open, and she immediately spotted him. Shirtless, he had his hands bracketed on the sink and was staring, into the mirror. It wasn't a good kind of staring either. He was obviously riled. At the shooter. At himself. At the world. At everything.

"This isn't a good time," he snarled.

"Yes, I know."

She didn't leave.

Carley stood there, their gazes connected in the

mirror. A thousand things passed between them. Things probably best left unsaid or unfelt. But it was too late for that. It was too late for a lot of things, including putting a leash on her own feelings.

Sloan's eyes narrowed slightly.

"You're playing with fire," he warned, his voice dark and raw.

"Is that supposed to send me running?" she challenged.

He took the challenge. Sloan pushed himself away from the sink and stormed toward her. Carley held her ground, and because she thought they could both use it, she tried to smile.

The smile didn't ease the tension. In fact, it seemed to increase it. Everything seemed to increase. Sloan's breathing. Her breathing, too. The energy that was zapping between them. The adrenaline.

And the need.

Especially the need.

Sloan reached out lightning-fast and caught onto the back of her. Carley didn't have time to react. He pulled her to him, and in the same motion his mouth was on hers. Nothing gentle. This was an assault. As if it were the first and last kiss he'd ever have.

Carley welcomed the heat. It rolled through her.

She kicked it up a notch. She put her arms around him and kissed him right back.

That seemed to be the only invitation Sloan

needed. He deepened the kiss, tightened the embrace. Building the sensations that had been barely under control for days.

He stopped, stared at her, his breath hot and racing. "If you're going to say no, say it now," Sloan insisted.

Carley managed to shake her head. "I'm not going to say no."

And to prove it, she started to strip off her shirt.

Chapter Fifteen

Carley's bra was pink.

Not a shocking shade of hot-pink. But a pale, barely there color that caught Sloan's attention and wouldn't let go.

That barely there part applied not just to the color but to the bra itself. Sheer lace. That was it. Sheer. Lace. She might as well have been wearing nothing, because he could see her breasts. And her nipples that were puckered and tight with arousal.

"Ignore the underwear," Carley insisted.

"Not on your life." In fact, it fulfilled a fantasy or two, and he was going to take full advantage of it.

Carley must have had some fantasies of her own in mind. Urgent ones. She reached for him. Sloan reached for her, too, and he kissed her until she went limp. The limpness didn't last long, though, because she quickly remembered that she had hands.

Agile, busy hands that began to undress them both.

Sloan knew he should be slowing down. He should be thinking this through. He should be weighing the consequences. But he also knew that thinking and weighing wouldn't help now. Carley and he were already past the point of no return. The only thing that was left was to finish what they'd started.

Until a single thought managed to make its way through the fog in his brain.

"I don't want to hurt you," he said, glancing down at her bandaged side.

"You won't. But I don't want to hurt you, either." She looked at his bandaged shoulder.

They were a pair, all right. Both injured and both hell bent on doing whatever it took to cool down this heat. Hopefully they wouldn't do any permanent damage before this was over.

"You won't hurt me," he assured her.

She obviously believed it, too, because she started to remove her pants. Sloan did stop her then, since there was something he wanted to do before they got naked. Because naked would lead to immediate sex.

The frantic need was already raging inside both of them. Their bodies certainly didn't require foreplay.

But he *wanted* the foreplay.

He wanted to give to Carley before he took her.

And he very much intended to take her.

Sloan grabbed both of her hands in one of his and

he lowered her zipper. That didn't stop the urgency within her. Nope. Carley moved against him. Her body squarely against his. And she had no trouble finding the most aroused part of him. She did a little maneuver with her hips that nearly caused his eyes to cross.

Not to be outdone, he rid her of her khakis and nearly had the breath knocked out of him when he saw her panties. Barely there pink. It matched the bra, and the lace only accented the triangle of dark hair beneath.

He went from being aroused to being ready to take her then and there.

Trying to keep things from getting out of control, Sloan unhooked the front clasp of her bra, and her breasts spilled out into his hand. She was perfect. And responsive, he soon learned. All it took was one taste of her right nipple, one flick of his tongue, and she was insisting they have sex against the wall.

Sloan was sort of insisting it, too.

"We might not survive this," Sloan mumbled, only partly joking.

She laughed. It was smoky and laced with nerves and a whole lot of need. She slid her leg along the outside of his, pulling him closer.

Her need fed his. Not good. There was already enough of that without adding more. But despite that need, that urgency, Sloan didn't rip off her panties and act like an animal. No. He wanted something that pure mindless sex wouldn't give him.

He wanted to watch Carley lose control.

And he wanted to be the one to cause it.

Ignoring the tug from his injury, Sloan pinned her against the wall. It didn't stop her from wriggling her hands out of his grip and going after his zipper. She likely would have succeeded if Sloan hadn't slid his hand down her stomach and into those pink panties.

She was hot, wet.

Ready.

And with just a touch from his fingers, she stopped the zipper quest.

A low, feminine sound rumbled in her throat. Her eyelids fluttered down. Her breath became heavy. And she moved. Mercy, did she ever move. Carley pushed the slick heat of her body against his fingers, and judging from the look of pure ecstasy on her face, she was savoring this.

Sloan savored it, too.

The feel of her. The taste of her mouth when he kissed her. Her aroused feminine scent that curled around him. Drowning him. It was a primal invitation for him to do what their bodies were begging them to do.

He continued to touch her, to stroke her, to move her closer and closer to the edge. Sloan could feel her that close. So close. So ready.

But then she stopped.

"I want you inside me," Carley said. And it wasn't a suggestion.

Pushing his hand aside, she reached into the medicine cabinet and extracted a foil-wrapped condom. She slapped it into the palm of his hand and tackled his zipper again. She didn't stop there. Nope. Carley kissed him. Hard and long. By the time he was out of his pants, they were pulling each other to the floor.

The *hard* tile floor.

Mindful of Carley's injury, Sloan knew this wasn't going to be a missionary thing. Ditto for her being on top, where she'd have to do too much work. He didn't want her exerting herself, even though she obviously had other ideas. She dragged off his boxers and went after *him.*

After a few clever strokes of her hand, Sloan knew he had to do something about the logistical problems caused by their injuries.

Carley protested it, of course, but Sloan lifted her back up against the wall. She said something about *now,* reached between them and squeezed him. It was a rather stark reminder—not that he needed it, of what she wanted.

"I don't want to hurt you," Sloan repeated, keeping his voice slow and easy. It was a hint for their bodies to do the same.

Still moving slowly, he put his mouth against her ear. He kissed her there. Just below her earlobe, and was pleased that it was an erogenous zone for her. Good. Because kissing her there fired his erogenous zones, as well.

She moaned, and her body became soft and pliable. So he continued to kiss her there while he slid his hand between her legs and touched her.

Her heartbeat and pulse were pounding, and he could feel it everywhere. Through both of them. His heart took on the rhythm of hers. The same cadence, The same intensity.

The same need.

"Sloan." She said his name like a plea.

Carley leaned the back of her head against the wall, pressing against him as he pressed against her. Soon, however, the slow, soft touching and the kissing weren't enough. Not nearly enough. Sloan leaned slightly away from her and managed to put on the condom.

"Sloan," she repeated.

He didn't make them wait any longer. He entered her slowly. Carefully. Savoring every inch of her as she was obviously savoring him.

The rhythm they found was as old as time. Stroke after stroke. Until the pace built. Until it was frantic. Until *they* were frantic.

Until the pleasure was unbearable.

"Sloan," she begged.

He understood what she wanted. What she needed. He pushed, hard, inside her. One last time.

And he felt her body close around him. Carley didn't go alone.

She took him with her while she whispered his name.

SATIATED AND EXHAUSTED, Carley went limp and together they slid to the floor. For several minutes she was so immersed in the aftermath of pleasure that it wasn't a bad position to be in—with Sloan still holding her close to him. With his groin still against her. But soon, too soon, the hard tile seemed to get cooler with each passing second.

Sloan must have sensed her discomfort—and her inability to move—because he slid beside her so that she could put her head on his shoulder.

He was slightly damp with sweat and smelled like sex. And his strong arms were warm and inviting. All in all, it was a good way to recover from what had just happened.

Of course, Carley couldn't leave that thought alone. It led to another.

What *had* just happened?

Obviously sex had happened.

But was that all?

She frowned, disgusted with herself that while she was still getting some orgasmic aftershocks, she was already trying to analyze their relationship. Or lack thereof. Because she had to accept that this might be nothing more than adrenaline sex.

Her frown deepened.

Sloan glanced down at her. "You're not having second thoughts?"

"No." But she had no idea if that was true or not.

"Then what's wrong?"

Carley looked up at him. "I was afraid you'd be this good."

His forehead bunched up. *"Afraid?"*

"You're a benchmark, Sloan." She paused when he shook his head. She didn't want to know what that head shake meant. No. She couldn't risk that now. In addition to feeling gloriously satisfied, she also felt ungloriously vulnerable.

It was best to go with something that wouldn't come back to haunt her later.

"I won't ever forget this," she said. Sheez. It sounded really stupid.

"I would hope not."

Now that sounded, well, promising. As if he were about to add something like he wouldn't forget it either. Or, better yet, he was very interested in re-peating the experience. And more. That this had been some kind of earth-moving revelation for him.

It certainly had been for her.

She frowned again. Obviously sex with Sloan had given her quite an imagination.

"I have my own theory about what creates good sex," Sloan said. He leaned in and kissed her. "It has to do with the people involved."

He didn't elaborate because a ringing sound echoed through the bathroom. Cursing and groaning, he reluctantly pulled away from her and located his discarded jeans. Carley sat back and enjoyed the view of a buck-naked Sloan locating his phone.

"Sgt. McKinney," Sloan snarled when he found it and answered the call.

Hating that they couldn't continue their conversation or attempt another round of lovemaking, Carley got up to dress. Probably because that call would involve work. Or even a visitor. She hoped it wasn't Zane. After glancing in the mirror, she knew there was no way she could completely erase that I-just-had-sex glow on her face.

She listened to Sloan's responses but couldn't figure out the caller. She couldn't tell, but she could determine other things. For one, it was something important, because Sloan put on his clothes as he talked.

Carley was completely dressed by the time he finished the call. "What happened?" she wanted to know.

"A lot, apparently. Until he can arrange for a safe house, Zane wants us to move to the police station. He's having cots delivered and he's beefing up the locks. That's where he wants us to spend the night— in the interrogation room."

"Why?" Carley asked.

"For one, he wants me to go through some old files that are stored in the basement."

"The ones that pertain to Lou Ann's murder?" Carley remembered discussing those with Zane not long after Zane had arrived in town.

Sloan nodded. "He thinks we've all missed something in those files. And Zane also wants us there because he just did a walk-through of the inn and decided it's the least secure building in the entire town. It's just not a good idea for us to stay here."

She couldn't argue with that, and while the killer—or at least someone—had attempted to break into the police station, he or she hadn't been able to gain access. Added to that, the interrogation room had no windows, so they couldn't be ambushed.

Carley stood there while Sloan gathered his gear. She waited for him to add something to their postcoital conversation. Not shop talk but personal talk.

He didn't.

She could tell from his stony expression that further conversation would have to wait. Carley only hoped that when they talked, she wouldn't blurt out that as much as she would have liked, this wasn't just sex for her.

She was falling hard for Sloan.

And her prediction?

The fall would be very painful.

Because once the case was solved, Sloan would leave town. And he'd also leave her with a broken heart.

Chapter Sixteen

"You should get some sleep," Sloan told Carley. He tipped his head to the green Army surplus cot that the deputy had delivered an hour earlier.

"Ditto," Carley answered, tipping her head to the matching cot on the other side of the room.

The deputy had obviously believed that Carley and he would want space—and lots of it—between them during the night.

Right.

Sloan had already violated that space and then some by making love to her in the bathroom of her apartment. He didn't regret it. No way. But he did regret that here he was thinking about doing it again and again. That was a dangerous path to take because every thought that he didn't devote solely to the killer could mean a delay in catching the bastard.

Carley returned her attention to the open manila folder on the table in front of her. Sloan didn't doubt that she was studying it with a lawman's eye. Heck, she even looked focused. Which was good. *Very good.* Talking about what'd happened between them wouldn't do a thing to make sure Carley was safe.

And that had to be Sloan's focus, too.

His obsession, if necessary.

The one thing he trusted was his ability as a Ranger. He was damn good at what he did—and he'd never needed that ability as much as he did now.

"Is there anything in that file?" Sloan asked. He grabbed one of the folders they'd retrieved from the basement, opened it and dropped down in the seat at the end of the table.

"Not so far. It's the interview that was done with Rosa Ramirez the night of Lou Ann's murder. Nothing jumps out at me so far. I'll keep reading."

Sloan scanned through his own file. It contained interviews of three of Leland's household staff. He'd already read through them once. So had Zane. So had Carley. So had countless other lawmen who'd tried to solve the sixteen-year-old murder. But Sloan tried again.

He failed almost immediately.

Huffing, he forced himself to reread the transcript of the recorded interview between the sheriff and Jennie Taylor, a maid who'd worked at Leland Hendricks's house. Judging from the woman's one-word responses, she hadn't been very cooperative.

"You seem, uh, restless," Carley said, not taking her eyes from the file.

"Angry," he corrected.

That caused her to lift her head and look in his direction. "About what?"

Their gazes met. Something unspoken passed between them. Carley wanted reassurance about the sex. Sloan could tell from her expression. But he couldn't give her that. The only thing he could do right now was the job.

And the job was Carley.

"Well?" she prompted.

"I'm angry about not being able to solve this case," he explained, knowing that wasn't what she wanted to hear and also knowing it wasn't what he wanted to say. "All we need is a break. One clue. If we get that, we can catch this killer."

She looked disappointed. For a moment. But she covered it by studying the notes again. "Maybe Zane will find gunshot residue on Leland or Donna's hands." She paused. "I know you barely got a glimpse of him, but was Leland wearing gloves when he was supposedly hiding behind my car?"

Sloan shook his head. "I couldn't tell. But he didn't have gloves or a gun by the time Zane and the deputies arrived on the scene."

"That's right, he didn't. When we raced into the inn, we lost sight of Leland," Carley continued. "He could have ditched both gloves and gun in the woods. Or my car."

"If he did, we'll find them." Sloan checked his

watch. It was still hours until daylight, but as soon as the sun came up, Zane would have a team out there, searching.

"Zane should probably question your mother, too," Carley added, her voice tentative.

Yes, because she'd visited them only minutes before the attack. She might have seen something. Sloan silently cursed. This was something he should have thought of sooner. It just proved how splintered his focus was right now.

"I was going to re-interview Stella about the night Lou Ann was killed, but Zane will automatically check our father's alibi," Sloan commented, thinking out loud.

If his father had an alibi, that is.

"I'm sure he will. But I think we need to concentrate on Leland and Donna. I don't see your father doing this," he heard Carley say. "He wouldn't shoot at you."

That was true. For all his father's faults, Sloan didn't think he'd attempt to kill his own son.

Of course, one could argue that those shots had not been aimed at him.

But at Carley.

Just the thought of that sent his blood raging again, and Sloan made a mental note to make sure his father did indeed have a legitimate alibi for the time of the shooting.

"What's that sound?" Carley asked.

Sloan pulled himself out of his thoughts and listened. It was faint, barely audible, but he heard it.

"It's like steam coming through a pipe," she added, getting to her feet.

It was, but Sloan knew in his gut that steam wasn't the cause. He hooked his arm around Carley and dragged her to the floor. It wasn't a second too soon.

The explosion tore though the building.

THE SOUND WAS DEAFENING, and the debris seemed to spew from every direction.

Something slammed into Carley's back. Hard. It knocked the breath from her and left her helpless, fighting for air.

Fighting for her life.

The room—or, rather, what was left of it—was suddenly dark. The explosion had no doubt caused them to lose power. Worse, the place was instantly filled with the scorched smell of smoke and dust particles.

Sloan turned and crawled over her, probably so he could shelter her with his body. Still, the debris pelted her legs and her head. She felt the sting of the cuts on her skin, but there was nothing she could do about it. Carley could only pray that Sloan wasn't being injured through all of this.

And that made her wonder—exactly what was *this?*

Obviously there'd been an explosion. But why? And who'd caused it?

The first thought that came to mind wasn't a good one. Had someone done this on purpose? It could be an accident, of course, but with the other things that'd been happening to Sloan and her, that didn't seem likely.

"Are you okay?" Sloan asked.

Carley tried to do an inventory. She had some minor injuries, no doubt about that, but she didn't feel as though anything had broken. "How about you?"

"I'll live. We have to get out of here," Sloan insisted. "The place is on fire."

"No one else is in the building, right?"

Sloan verified. "Right." And that was the only good thing about their situation.

He moved off her, and Carley rolled to the side. Well, she rolled as much as she could considering the entire floor was covered with rubble. A good chunk of the ceiling had also broken loose and was literally dangling over them.

Sloan reacted fast. He caught onto her, rolling them over the debris just as the ceiling came crashing down.

More dust. It was smothering. As was the smoke. Carley batted it away with her hand and spotted the orange-red flames eating their way through the interior wall. Sloan was right. They had to get out of there.

But how?

Sloan got to his feet, dragging her with him. Carley frantically looked around for an escape route. She forced herself to remain calm. She couldn't panic.

"We can't get out through the hall," Sloan informed her.

Carley soon saw why. The hall was already engulfed in flames and thick black smoke that was snaking straight toward them.

The room had no windows. Ironically that was the reason they'd chosen it—so the would-be killer couldn't gun them down while they were working. But the killer had obviously found a different way to get rid of them.

"We're not going to die," Sloan snarled.

Carley wanted to agree with that, but it wasn't looking good. Her body reacted to that, too. Her heart was racing and her breath was much too fast and thin.

"We'll take off our shirts," he instructed. "We can put them over our faces while we make a run for it."

It wasn't a good plan, and judging from the anxiousness in Sloan's voice, he knew that. They'd be burned alive if they went into the hall.

Of course, the same would happen if they stayed put.

She coughed when a gust of smoke washed over her and she batted away the smoke and the heat so she could see. Her gaze landed on the far wall.

"There was once a window there," Carley said, pointing to it.

Sloan didn't waste even a second. He picked up a chair. The drywall was already battered and bashed, thanks to the explosion, so it didn't take much effort for him to start tearing his way through it.

Carley grabbed the first thing she could find—a piece of the door—and she began to ram it into the wall. With them working together, the remainder of the drywall gave way. Behind it was the window, covered by a shutter.

The smoke became thicker, and Carley could feel the heat of the fire pressing against their backs. She risked looking over her shoulder and didn't like what she saw. The flames were not only higher, they were closing in on them.

Sloan struggled to open the window.

It was stuck.

Stuck!

Carley cursed and bashed it with the door piece. Anger flared through her, and it was as hot and lethal as the fire. She would not die here. Nor would Sloan. Somehow they would make it out alive so they could catch the person responsible for this.

Probably because there wasn't enough room and because he was stronger, Sloan pushed her aside and rammed the chair through what was left of the glass panes. He didn't stop there. He punched and clawed his way through the window frame and to the shutter.

Carley could feel her heart in her throat. Every inch of her was pulsing with adrenaline and tension. She prayed that someone had heard the explosion and called the fire department. Hopefully someone was already on the way.

But they had to do something in the meantime.

She pulled in a breath, but it was filled with smoke. Her lungs were on fire. Starved for air. Because she wasn't sure how much longer she could last, she bashed her hands against the shutters.

The wooden shutters finally caved in.

As did the wall behind them.

Sparks, embers and more smoke spewed right at them.

Sloan latched on to her arm and practically shoved her through the opening. Carley gladly went through and took a much-needed breath of air, but not before she reached for Sloan and helped him through.

"We can't stay by the building," he managed to say, though he was coughing. "The whole place is about to come down."

He was right, but it took Carley a moment to get her legs to cooperate. Sloan helped. He took her by the wrist, and they started to run toward the clearing that fronted the woods.

Carley ignored the stabbing pain in her side. She

ignored her breath-starved body. And she ran as if her life depended on it.

Because it did.

She heard the groaning sound behind her. Not human. It was the sound of the police station succumbing to the fire.

Sloan stopped and pulled her to him. Probably to shelter her from the flying sparks and debris. She could feel his heart pounding as hard as hers.

"This wasn't an accident," she said.

"No." He took in several deep breaths. "We have to find a phone and make sure someone's called the fire department."

Sloan turned to take them in the direction of the inn, but then he stopped.

"What's wrong?" Carley asked.

He didn't answer. He didn't have to. She followed his gaze. His eyes were focused on the woods.

Carley must have seen the movement at the same time Sloan did because together they dropped to the ground.

As the bullet came right over their heads.

Chapter Seventeen

It was too risky to pull Carley to the ground and hunker down. The fire from the explosion was about to bring the building down around them. They also couldn't just stay put. So Sloan took out his gun and shoved Carley into the woods that butted up against the police station. Carley followed suit and drew her own weapon.

Another shot. It was fired from a gun rigged with a silencer.

It came too damn close.

And that close shot riled Sloan to the core. How the hell had he let this happen again? He should have done something, anything, to keep Carley safe. Instead here she was, right back in harm's way.

Keeping low, Sloan maneuvered them toward a thick cluster of trees that was on the opposite end from where those shots originated. If the killer could use the thick woods for cover and concealment, so could they.

"Who's doing this?" Carley whispered.

"I don't know." But he intended to find out.

Once he had Carley safe, that is.

He couldn't put her at further risk.

Sloan positioned her to the side of a sprawling oak and he followed right behind her, using his body to shield her as best he could.

"I can't return fire like this," she reminded him. It was also likely a reminder that she didn't need kid-glove protection.

Tough. She was getting it anyway. Sloan knew he wouldn't be able to live with himself if something happened to her.

"If it becomes necessary for you to return fire," he whispered, "then I'll move." But he figured that wouldn't happen anytime soon.

Carley huffed, but she stayed put. Mainly because he didn't give her a choice. Sloan pinned her in place so that he could protect her.

"Do you see anyone?" she snarled.

Sloan didn't answer right away. He took a moment to comb the woods around them. And he listened. Because it would be almost impossible for a killer to walk through the woodsy debris without them hearing him or her.

At least Sloan hoped that was true.

"I don't see anything," he said putting his mouth directly against Carley's ear.

He must have tempted fate, because he'd no

sooner finished saying that when there was another shot. Then another. Both bullets slammed into the oak, tearing through the bark.

Sloan didn't move. Didn't make a sound. Though he was concerned that both Carley and he were breathing loudly enough to be heard. It couldn't be helped, though. The escape from the explosion had left them both out of breath and ragged from the spent adrenaline. Of course, he hadn't counted on a double attack tonight.

If that's what this was.

Maybe the explosion and these silenced shots weren't the work of the same person. Of course, it was entirely possible they were. And that meant someone was deadly serious about trying to murder them.

Overkill, indeed.

There was another shot. Then a fourth. This one didn't go into the tree. Instead it went just to the right of them. That meant the gunman was on the move.

And Sloan hadn't heard the movement.

It also meant Carley and he could be ambushed.

That brought on another surge of anger. He was tired of this sick game. Tired of being on the receiving end of those bullets.

"Don't move," he warned Carley.

Sloan did a split-second calculation of point of origin of that last shot and leaned out of cover. Just a fraction. Just enough for him to get off a clear shot. He took aim and fired.

And fired again.

Unlike the silenced shots, his blasted through the otherwise quiet woods. Those blasts were quickly joined by another sound.

Sirens.

Someone had apparently alerted the Justice fire department. Thank God. At a minimum, they could stop the blaze from spreading to other buildings. As an added bonus, the sirens might scare the shooter away.

"Listen," Carley said. "Do you hear it?"

Because Sloan didn't think she was referring to the sirens, and because her body tensed completely, he tried to sift through the sounds. The crackle of the fire. The building collapsing bit by bit. And, yes, the sirens. He could hear no voices, but he thought he might have heard some kind of movement.

Hurried footsteps, maybe.

"The person's coming closer," Carley concluded.

She wriggled herself away from the tree and took aim. Sloan silently cursed her choice of action, but he had to go along with it. It might be the only way to save themselves from being killed.

He just hoped he didn't regret it.

Sloan put his back to hers and angled his body slightly so that he could cover the north and west portion of the woods. Carley took the south.

They stood there. Breaths held. Hearts racing. Waiting. For a sound or some other indication of where and when to fire their own shots.

The sirens screamed closer, and the intensity of the sound seemed to set the rhythm of his heartbeat. He wasn't scared. Not for himself, anyway. But he was worried about Carley. She'd been through so much and she apparently had even more to go through. Despite the impending arrival of the fire department, Carley and he literally weren't out of the woods yet.

Seconds passed. Slowly. The fire truck stopped on the street in front of what was left of the police station. Sloan glanced at it. But it wasn't a good time for such a glance.

The bullets returned.

Three shots. Rapid succession.

Three shots.

All slammed through the woods and came right at them. Specifically all came right at Carley.

Carley returned fire.

Sloan turned to do the same, but the sudden overwhelming sensation had him changing his mind.

Something was wrong.

Sloan slung his arm around Carley's waist and hurriedly dragged her to the ground.

The next bullet slammed into the thin air where Carley had just stood. Another second, another fraction of an inch, and she would have been killed.

Carley obviously grasped that concept.

Her breath shattered, but she didn't just lie there and accept it. She came up, preparing to fire. And likely would have.

If Sloan hadn't stopped her.

He totally understood her need to get this person who was responsible. But it was paltry compared to his need to keep her alive and safe.

"No!" Carley shouted, trying to fight him off.

Sloan didn't let go because he knew with this rage storming inside her that she would no doubt go in pursuit. While it was something he wanted to do, he couldn't let that negate common sense.

So Sloan held on to Carley while she struggled to get free. Behind them, he heard the shouts of the firemen who were already battling the blaze.

He also heard something that robbed him of a few years.

Sloan heard the voices of some people from the town. Frantic shouts. Bystanders who'd come out to see what'd happened.

Bystanders who could be shot and killed by stray bullets.

He prayed that the gunman was finished for the night. Not just for the bystanders but for Carley, who was still struggling to get up.

Despite the noise and activity, Sloan forced himself to concentrate on only one thing.

The shooter.

Was the person still out there, ready to fire?

If so, he didn't hear footsteps. Nor did he see anyone moving around in the woods.

"You should have let me go," Carley mumbled.

Just like that, she gave up her struggle. Probably because she also realized the gunman was gone.

"No, I shouldn't have."

"Don't you understand?" Her voice was nothing but pure, raw emotion. As was the stark expression on her face when she rolled over to face him. "We could have ended it here, *now!*"

Sloan pointed to the bullet embedded in the tree. "And you could have been killed. Do you have any idea how close that last shot came to your head?"

Now it was his turn to express some emotion. His voice was strained and burning. Just the way he felt.

She stared at him, blinking hard.

"I had no intention of losing you tonight," he said, just in case she needed any more clarification. "I won't trade your life for an arrest, got that?"

And he didn't leave room for argument.

Carley blinked again. "I understand. I feel the same way about you." She immediately looked away, dodging his gaze, looking everywhere but at him. "You saved my life tonight. Thank you."

"You're welcome. And don't worry, I won't tell anyone." When he snared her gaze, he winked at her.

"Don't joke. Not now." With her gun still clutched in her hand, she slipped her arm around his neck. Her face touched his, and that's when Sloan felt her tears.

Because she was trembling and because he

wanted to hold her, Sloan pulled her to him. It didn't last long. Mere seconds. They pulled away from each other and took aim again, when they heard the voice.

"Sloan?" someone called out.

He turned and spotted Deputy Luis Spinoza making his way toward them. "You two all right?" the deputy asked.

"We've been better," Carley answered. Sloan got to his feet, caught onto her arm and helped her to hers.

The deputy nodded and then glanced over his shoulder. Not a furtive, uneasy glance, but it still conveyed that he wasn't comfortable. "Your mother's here."

It took Sloan a moment to realize the deputy was talking to him and not Carley. "Stella's here?"

"Yeah."

"Why?" Carley and Sloan asked in unison.

The deputy shrugged. "We found her sitting by the side of the sheriff's office. She's pretty shaken, Sloan, and she says she's not leaving until she talks to you."

Chapter Eighteen

Sloan stood at the front entrance of the inn and tried to decide what to do. Not about his mother. He knew what he had to do about her—he had to go see what she wanted.

It was Carley that was the issue.

She stood behind him, occasionally making huffing sounds, and she was more than a little upset that he wanted to leave her behind while he visited Stella.

"What she has to say could be related to the case," Carley reminded him.

He glanced over his shoulder at her to let her know he wasn't buying that argument. "This is my mother. She probably wants to browbeat me just in case I have any notion of trying to question my father."

"If that's all she wanted, then why didn't she wait until at least the fire was put out?"

It was the billon-dollar question, but then, logic wasn't always at play when it came to his mother.

"I'd feel better if you stayed put," he told Carley.

"I'd feel better if *you* stayed put," she countered. "There's no reason to do this face-to-face. You can talk to Stella on the phone."

True, but something told Sloan this was best done in person. Despite his assurances to Carley that this would probably be a browbeating meeting, Sloan really didn't believe that.

Something was wrong.

But what?

Was it linked the murders? To the explosion? To his father? Or was this truly Stella being Stella?

There was only way to find out. Sloan had to see her. Carley apparently felt the same way. If he left her behind, he'd worry about her every minute. Because maybe the killer was watching. Waiting. For Sloan to leave Carley alone so he or she could go after her again.

A truly sickening thought.

At least if Carley was with him, he could protect her. Well, maybe. He hadn't exactly done a stellar job with that so far. Worse, he'd complicated the hell out of things by making love to her.

And it was a complication.

The kind that could cause a man to lose focus. In this case, that could be fatal for both of them.

Still, there was no way he could go back and undo things. The only thing he could do was proceed forward and solve this case. Putting a killer behind bars was the only way he could keep Carley safe.

"All right," Sloan grumbled, turning toward her. "You can come. But, so help me, Carley, you better not take any unnecessary chances."

That pert chin came up. "And neither will you."

Semisatisfied that they'd both gotten their points across, Sloan motioned for Luis Spinoza, the deputy, to go with them, and Carley stepped out when they did. In fact, she fell in step right alongside him, with the deputy following behind. All three of them drew their weapons.

"I'd really prefer that you not be out here in the open," Sloan said to her.

It didn't do any good.

"Well, I don't want you out here, either." Carley glanced around them.

He cursed under his breath. This wasn't good. Each wanted the other to stay tucked away. Where it was safe. But in their line of work, safety wasn't always an option.

His brain knew that. So did hers.

But their hearts weren't in tune with the logic.

"See what sex does?" he mumbled. "It makes us crazy."

She made a sound of agreement. "You regret it?"

"No." Sloan said it so quickly and with so much emotion that he decided to take a moment to level his voice. "But I regret what it's done to us."

He glanced at her to see how she was taking that. She obviously wasn't taking it well. Probably because Carley didn't know what to make of a comment like that.

Sloan didn't know what to make of it, either.

Nor would he figure it out. Not now, anyway. There wasn't time. He spotted the remains of the police station just ahead. And amid all that still-smoking rubble he spotted his mother. Stella was sitting on the ash-layered curb just a few yards away from what was left of the front door.

Stella looked up when he approached her, and Sloan had no trouble seeing her reddened eyes. That wasn't his only indication that something was wrong. His mother's hair was disheveled and her hands were trembling.

"Mom, what are you doing here?" he asked when he reached her.

She looked away, staring at the empty street, and for a moment Sloan didn't think she would answer.

"Mrs. McKinney?" Carley greeted.

Stella didn't look at her either. Instead his mother shook her head and plowed her hands into the sides of her hair. "I can't live with this anymore."

All right. That didn't do much to steady Sloan's nerves. "What do you mean?"

"This." Stella slid one of her hands over her heart. "I can't live with what I know."

Since this sounded like something both of them might have trouble hearing, Sloan eased down on the curb beside her. "Is this about the explosion?"

"It's about everything." Stella moistened her lips. "I didn't tell the truth about what happened all those years ago. The night Lou Ann was murdered."

Obviously intrigued, Carley came closer.

"You can tell the truth now," Sloan assured his mother.

Stella nodded. "But you aren't going to like it." And with that, she turned her tear-filled eyes toward him.

"I'm listening," Sloan promised. And he was praying, too. Praying that he could accept whatever his mother was about to say.

"That night, I went after Jim to try to stop him from seeing Lou Ann," Stella said as if it left a bad taste in her mouth. "Lou Ann was a very bad woman. She didn't care about our family. She didn't care what she was doing to me."

Sloan cleared his throat when his mother didn't continue. "Did you do something about that, Mom?"

Stella nodded. "I called her. Told her to stop."

"That's all you did—you called Lou Ann?"

"Yes."

Sloan hadn't realized that he'd been holding his breath until his lungs started to ache. "Calling her wasn't a crime, Mom. Many women in your position would have done the same thing."

Or worse.

Much worse.

"Your father came home that night," Stella continued.

That did away with any relief he'd gotten from her previous comments. "Of course he came home," Sloan added.

"Your father and I talked," Stella said as if she hadn't even heard Sloan. "He was drunk and he reeked of that woman and her thick, cheap perfume. We argued. I even slapped him. And that's when he told me."

Carley touched his arm. Rubbed gently. Trying to soothe him. It didn't help. Sloan felt as if his world was about to come tumbling down.

"What did your husband tell you, Mrs. McKinney?" Carley asked.

Stella looked past him and her gaze connected with Carley. "I asked him if he'd broken off things with Lou Ann, and he said yes, that he may have broken them off permanently."

"He was drunk," Sloan interjected.

His mother kept her attention focused on Carley. "Jim said he thought he'd killed her."

That hit Sloan like a heavyweight's punch. He couldn't catch his breath. He got to his feet somehow, but once he'd stood, he had no idea what to do.

"Mrs. McKinney, could you come back to the inn with me so I can take your statement?" Carley asked.

Stella didn't answer.

"Mrs. McKinney?" Carley pressed. "Are you all right?"

His mother didn't say a word. Stella hugged her knees to her chest and began to rock. She no longer was focused on Carley. She didn't appear to be focused on anything.

"I'm so sorry," Carley whispered to him.

She reached for him, but Sloan stepped away. Though she meant well, he couldn't handle that kind of compassion right now. One thing was for sure— he had to get out of there. He had to think.

He had to breathe.

Hell.

He had to have answers.

Was his father a killer after all?

CARLEY ADJUSTED HER position on the bed in the "safe house." Or, rather, the upscale Dallas condo that qualified as a Rangers safe house. And she tossed and turned again.

And again.

It was futile. Sleep was out of the question. Yet, when Sloan had gotten her settled into the condo in the wee hours of the morning, she'd promised him that she would at least rest and let the medics check her for injuries. She'd done the latter, only after he'd assured her that he would do the same, but sleep and rest were things she couldn't control.

At the time she'd made the promise to rest, Carley knew it was one she couldn't keep, but she'd wanted to do everything within her power to relieve some of Sloan's stress. After all, he'd just received a bomb-shell. He'd heard his mother admit that Jim McKinney had possibly murdered his former lover, Lou Ann, and then Sloan had had to watch an ambulance take his mother for a psychiatric evaluation at the hospital.

That was way too much for one person to deal with. Hence her assurance that she'd do whatever Sloan had asked—which was get some rest and stay put, even if that meant she could no longer be actively involved in the investigation. She'd made that promise as Sloan had given her a mechanical kiss on the cheek and reminded her that there was a diligent, highly qualified Ranger in the living room who'd keep watch.

Then Sloan had walked away.

And Carley had let him.

It hadn't been easy. Actually, it had been one of the hardest things she'd ever done. But it was necessary. Sloan needed time and space. He had to come to terms with what he'd just learned.

If that was even possible.

How did a man come to terms with the fact that the father he loved might be a killer?

Worse, it went deeper than that. His mother had kept the secret all these years. She'd lied by omission, and it was a doozy of a lie. And it all made Carley think.

Just how far did this go?

If Jim McKinney had indeed killed Lou Ann, then had he killed Sarah Wallace, as well?

Had Jim been the cloaked person who'd tried to kill Sloan and her? Had he been responsible for that explosion and fire that they'd barely escaped?

That brought on a new round of tossing and turning. Carley finally gave up, got out of bed and headed to the kitchen. She passed the Ranger along the way, who issued a crisp good morning. Carley refrained from barking, *What's so good about it?*

When she reached the kitchen, she went straight for the freezer and located something that interested her. Caramel-fudge ice cream might give her a little solace. She grabbed the carton and a spoon and sat down at the table.

The ice cream tasted like sugary chalk in her mouth. Worse, everything felt awful. Out of kilter. And it likely wouldn't get any better until they knew the truth.

It sickened her to think of the possibility of Sloan's father as a killer. It would have taken a cold-blooded monster to do what that cloaked figure had done. Especially if he'd done it to his own son.

Of course, there was a flip side to this. Sloan had kept his own secret about his mother possibly not being home that night. So maybe Stella's confession was meant to throw the guilt off her.

It hadn't worked.

Carley added the woman to the list of suspects:

Donna, Leland, Jim and Stella. Somehow Sloan and she had to figure out who it was, because things couldn't continue like this. That said, they didn't seem close to bringing a killer to justice. That wouldn't get easier with Sloan having to divide his attention between the case and his mother.

An added complication was what had happened between Sloan and her.

Sloan was right. Sex did change things. But it didn't always change things for the better. He'd walked away from her tonight because there literally wasn't time for anything personal.

There might never be.

Both of them were focused on their careers. On the case. Doing a good job was as bone-deep to them as their DNA. They couldn't change what they were, who they were, and maybe that would always stand in the way of anything deeper developing between them.

Carley closed the lid on the ice cream and tossed the spoon into the sink. As the spoon clanged against the stainless steel, she felt the first tear form in her eye.

It was a sad day in a woman's life when she started lying to herself. Her job, her DNA, the case wouldn't stand in the way of something deeper developing between Sloan and her.

Well, it wouldn't stand in the way as far as she was concerned.

Because she'd already fallen hard for Sloan McKinney. And not just fallen.

She was in love with him.

And somehow she had to live with the likelihood that Sloan would never love her in return.

Chapter Nineteen

Sloan checked once again to make sure he hadn't been followed.

He hadn't been.

Even now, security was one of his main concerns. He hoped it wouldn't be much longer. Of course, Carley would have some say in that.

After a brief mental lecture, he marched up to the door of the condo, lifted his hand to ring the bell— and froze. Just froze.

There was so much at stake.

Too much.

He had some tough news to tell Carley and he didn't know how she would react to it. Sloan hated the thought of seeing disappointment and hurt on her face, but there was no way to avoid this. He had to tell her.

He couldn't leave things as they were any longer.

Sloan rang the bell, and the door flew open. He was greeted by Sgt. Mark Meadows, a rather harried-looking fellow Ranger, who had his gun drawn. The sight of that gun sent Sloan's heart racing out of control.

"Is Carley all right?" Sloan demanded, pushing his way past Meadows.

"She's just fine. But thank God you're here," Meadows grumbled. He grabbed Sloan's arm and practically pulled him around to face him.

"What's wrong?" Sloan asked.

"You mean other than the fact that Carley asks every five minutes when she'll be able to leave? And she keeps pestering me for an update about the investigation. In between those particular questions, she keeps asking if you've called. So, other than her driving me crazy, nothing's wrong."

Sloan relaxed a little. He'd expected Carley to be impatient and even demanding and he had prayed some big-time prayers that it was all she would do. It could have been worse. She could have ditched her promise to stay put and returned to Justice.

But she hadn't.

For two whole days she'd stayed shut inside the tiny Dallas condo, and Sloan figured she was pushing the limits of sanity for herself and the Ranger guard. It was certainly questioning *his* sanity, and he hadn't been the one stuck in the safe house.

"Why don't you take a lunch break?" Sloan suggested. "I need to talk to Carley."

He didn't have to suggest it twice. Sgt. Meadows

grabbed his things and headed out. Sloan took a deep breath, bracing himself for what he'd come here to do.

"Carley?" he called out, double locking the door behind him. He also reset the elaborate security system.

He heard the footsteps almost immediately. Carley came barreling out of the bedroom. She was dressed in her sheriff's uniform, complete with shoulder holster and badge, and she looked ready to report for duty.

She stopped just a few feet away from him and offered a tentative smile. That smile vanished when she noted the expression on his face.

"It's bad news," she said.

"Good and bad," Sloan confirmed.

She nodded and moistened her lips. "Start with the good. It might soften the bad."

Sloan didn't think it would, but he proceeded anyway. "Early next week you'll get a call from the Rangers selection committee."

"I will?" She flattened her hand on her chest as if to steady her heart.

"You will."

She waited a moment, and he could see that she was fighting to keep her composure. The nerves were there, barely beneath the surface. "And it'll be *good* news?"

"You bet. But since I'm not supposed to be telling you this, you'll need to act surprised when the captain congratulates you and informs you that you're going to be a Texas Ranger."

Carley didn't move. She didn't react. She just stood there, staring at him.

"Did you hear me?" Sloan asked.

She nodded, and probably because she no longer seemed too steady on her feet, she felt behind her for the sofa and then sank down onto it.

"I can't believe it," she mumbled. "It happened. It really happened. It's a dream come true."

Sloan released the breath he'd been holding. She still wanted to be a Ranger. That was good. He only hoped that the news would soften the blow of what he had to say next.

"You'll have to go to training, of course," he continued. Best to focus only on the positive for now. She needed time for it to sink in and to savor it. "You won't have any trouble with the curriculum."

Carley's eyes widened and she shook her head. "But what about my job in Justice?"

"I've been looking into some possibilities. When your selection is officially announced, I'll let the mayor and the D.A. know that there's a deputy over in Cahill who's interested in the job."

"Deputy Jeff Brewer," she supplied. "Yes, I know him. He's a good man."

"And he's very interested in wearing the sheriff's badge. You won't mind handing over the reins to someone else while you're fulfilling your destiny?"

"My destiny," she repeated, still not sounding overly enthused. "Yes, I guess that is my destiny. Being a lawman 24-7."

Carley looked up at him. Stared deeply into his eyes. She opened her mouth to say something, but Sloan interrupted her. He recognized that look. She wanted to have a heart-to-heart, and he wasn't ready for that yet.

"After your training, there's an extremely good chance that you'll be assigned to the Dallas area," he continued.

"In your company?"

He nodded. "It looks that way."

She continued to stare at him. "Well, since you're not smiling and since you're obviously not happy about that, let me just go ahead and clear the air. No," she said when he tried to interrupt her again. "I can't stand tiptoeing around this."

"I'm sorry," Sloan said because he didn't know what else to say.

"Yeah. Well, I'm sorry, too. I could get all stoic and pretend that it doesn't matter, but it does. It matters a lot. It wasn't just sex for me, Sloan, but I understand that's all it was for you."

It took him a moment to figure out what she was saying and another moment to remember how to speak. "What?"

She frowned. Her stare intensified. "What do you mean *what?*"

"I mean *what,* as in *what* the heck are you talking about?"

Carley put her palms up. "I'm talking about giving you an out. You didn't have to come here to soften the blow of dumping me. A phone call would have sufficed."

Sloan was surprised that he didn't keel over from shock. "That's not why I came here."

"Oh, good news/bad news," she said, sarcasm lacing her voice. "It's like good cop/bad cop. Very effective with hotheads like Leland and Donna, but it isn't going to be so effective with me. Not when it comes to this subject. Just be direct. Get the dumping over with."

"I didn't come here to dump you. I came here to tell you that I'd failed."

Now it was Carley who looked ready to keel over from shock. "How did you fail?"

"Are you ready for a list?" He held up one finger. "I couldn't get my mother to talk. If she knows anything, she's keeping it to herself." He lifted another finger. "My father has no alibi for the time of the explosion and isn't talking, either." A third finger went up. "And after working nonstop for the past forty-eight hours, I've made absolutely zero progress in catching this killer. I haven't even been able to find a trail for the money Donna was supposedly going to use to pay off Lou Ann."

The seconds passed. Slowly. Crawling by. While

Sloan waited for Carley to show all the frustration and anger that had to be bottled inside her.

But it didn't exactly go down that way.

She laughed.

Really laughed.

In fact, she laughed so hard there were tears in her eyes. Sloan could only stand there and look confused, because he didn't have a clue what was going on.

"That's why you look as if you're the bearer of doom and gloom?" she asked. "Because you haven't made progress on the case?"

"I failed to catch a killer," Sloan reminded her, poking his thumb against his chest. "A killer who keeps trying to kill you."

"A killer who's evaded authorities for sixteen years," Carley reminded him right back. "Good grief, Sloan, I didn't expect you to come here and tell me that there'd been an arrest. That would have been nice, true, but it would have definitely been unexpected."

Okay. That made him relax a little, but he was still confused. "So you're not upset?"

"Not about that. But I am furious with myself for making that girlie confession about it not just being sex for me. Talk about something I'll never live down."

Even though she was frustrated and perhaps a little embarrassed, Sloan felt himself completely relax. Finally he was no longer confused. He dragged over an ottoman and sat down across from her.

"You know what I've been dreaming about?" he asked.

"No." And she didn't ask about what, either. She seemed to be stewing now, and he thought he knew why.

"I've been dreaming about sex with you," he explained. "Specifically old-fashioned, me-on-top sex. And you-on-top. Basically the positions are negotiable."

She relaxed a little. In fact, she smiled. Not a sarcastic kind of I'm-embarrassed smile. Carley obviously liked the idea of having sex with him.

"I've been dreaming about that, too," she admitted. "I don't suppose there'll be a problem with two Rangers having a hot, torrid sexual relationship?"

"None whatsoever."

Because Sloan couldn't wait, he leaned closer and kissed her. The taste of her rolled through him. It was so good that he hauled her to him and kissed her again.

"How about good old-fashioned sofa sex?" she asked. "Is that a possibility?"

"Definitely. In a minute."

Carley didn't want to wait that minute. She began to unbutton his shirt.

Sloan let her do just that while he continued. "In addition to having sex with you, I've been thinking about destiny. My destiny. Yours. Ours."

"Uh-huh," she said as if she weren't really paying attention. That was probably because she had gotten his shirt open and was kissing his chest.

Since it was easier to concentrate with her not doing that, Sloan opened her shirt. He found a pink silk bra that had him smiling. And he dropped some tongue kisses on the tops of her breasts. It worked. Carley made some sounds of pleasure and melted against him.

In situations like this, hot and melted was just how he wanted her. It might make her more agreeable when he dropped the next bombshell.

"Personally I think our destinies are on the same path," he mumbled against her right breast.

Another mindless uh-huh. Sloan climbed onto the sofa with her, eased her onto the cushions and kissed his way down her stomach. He enjoyed himself for several moments and then he put things on hold.

She blinked, stared at him. "Why did you stop?"

"So I can get to the gist of this visit."

"The *gist*," she repeated, making it sound very naughty. "I'll bet you know where my gist is."

He would reward her for that naughtiness later.

Sloan cupped her chin so they'd have eye contact. "After you finish your training and become a Ranger,

I'm going to ask you to marry me. Since I'm giving you so much advance notice, you can act surprised when the moment comes."

And he waited.

Breath held.

He'd sounded light enough. Even a little cocky. But he had no idea how Carley was going to take a proposal.

"Marry you?" she questioned.

He nodded. His air-starved lungs started to ache, but he didn't breathe. Couldn't breathe. All he could do was wait for Carley to deliver the verdict.

"Why do you want to marry me?" she asked. Easing away from him, she sat up.

"Good question. Easy answer. It's because it wasn't just sex for me, either. I'm in love with you."

"You love me?" she repeated.

Before the last word left her mouth, there were tears in her eyes. He was pretty sure they were good tears, but just in case, Sloan went back to holding his breath.

"I love you, too," she said.

Sloan had no doubts that she meant it, because Carley launched herself at him and kissed him as if he were, well, her destiny.

"I mean, I *really* love you." Her eyes sparkled.

Sloan had to blink back some tears of his own. This was going far better than he'd ever imagined. In fact, this was as good at it got.

Almost.

There was something he was still waiting to hear.

"So let me repeat myself," he said. "When you finish your training, I'm going to ask you to marry me."

Carley slid her arms around his neck. "And what will you do when I say yes?"

Relieved, happy and aware that he was the luckiest man on earth, Sloan kissed her. "I'll act very surprised."

* * * * *

Don't miss the heart-stopping conclusion
of The Silver Star of Texas,
when the murderer will finally be revealed.
Look for Rita Herron's
JUSTICE FOR A RANGER
in March 2007,
only from Harlequin Intrigue!

Happily ever after is just the beginning…

Turn the page for a sneak preview of
A HEARTBEAT AWAY
by
Eleanor Jones

Harlequin Everlasting—Every great love
has a story to tell. ™
A brand-new series from Harlequin Books

Special? A prickle ran down my neck and my heart started to beat in my ears. Was today really special?

"Tuck in," he ordered.

I turned my attention to the feast that he had spread out on the ground. Thick, home-cooked-ham sandwiches, sausage rolls fresh from the oven and a huge variety of mouthwatering scones and pastries. Hunger pangs took over, and I closed my eyes and bit into soft homemade bread.

When we were finally finished, I lay back against the bluebells with a groan, clutching my stomach.

Daniel laughed. "Your eyes are bigger than your stomach," he told me.

I leaned across to deliver a punch to his arm, but he rolled away, and when my fist met fresh air I collapsed in a fit of giggles before relaxing on my back and staring up into the flawless blue sky. We lay like that for quite a while, Daniel and I, side by side in companionable silence, until he stretched out his hand in an arc that encompassed the whole area.

"Don't you think that this is the most beautiful place in the entire world?"

His voice held a passion that echoed my own feelings, and I rose onto my elbow and picked a buttercup to hide the emotion that clogged my throat.

"Roll over onto your back," I urged, prodding him with my forefinger. He obliged with a broad grin, and I reached across to place the yellow flower beneath his chin.

"Now, let us see if you like butter."

When a yellow light shone on the tanned skin below his jaw, I laughed.

"There…you do."

For an instant our eyes met, and I had the strangest sense that I was drowning in those honey-brown depths. The scent of bluebells engulfed me. A roaring filled my ears, and then, unexpectedly, in one smooth movement Daniel rolled me onto my back and plucked a buttercup of his own.

"And do *you* like butter, Lucy McTavish?" he asked. When he placed the flower against my skin, time stood still.

His long lean body was suspended over mine, pinning me against the grass. Daniel…dear, comfortable, familiar Daniel was suddenly bringing out in me the strangest sensations.

"Do you, Lucy McTavish?" he asked again, his voice low and vibrant.

My eyes flickered toward his, the whisper of a sigh escaped my lips and although a strange lethargy had crept into my limbs, I somehow felt as if all my nerve endings were on fire. He felt it, too—I could see it in his warm brown eyes. And when he lowered his face to mine, it seemed to me the most natural thing in the world.

None of the kisses I had ever experienced could have even begun to prepare me for the feel of Daniel's lips on mine. My entire body floated on a tide of ecstasy that shut out everything but his soft, warm mouth, and I knew that this was what I had been waiting for the whole of my life.

"Oh, Lucy." He pulled away to look into my eyes. "Why haven't we done this before?"

Holding his gaze, I gently touched his cheek, then I curled my fingers through the short thick hair at the base of his skull, overwhelmed by the longing to drown again in the sensations that flooded our bodies. And when his long tanned fingers crept across my tingling skin, I knew I could deny him nothing.

* * * * *

Be sure to look for A HEARTBEAT AWAY,
available February 27, 2007.
And look, too, for THE DEPTH OF LOVE
by Margot Early,
the story of a couple who must learn
that love comes in many guises—
and in the end it's the only thing that counts.

HARLEQUIN® *Romance*.

From reader-favorite

MARGARET WAY

Cattle Rancher, Convenient Wife

On sale March 2007.

**"Margaret Way delivers...
vividly written, dramatic stories."**
—*Romantic Times BOOKreviews*

---

*For more wonderful wedding stories,
watch for Patricia Thayer's new miniseries
starting in April 2007.*

Rocky Mountain
BRIDES

Hearts racing
Blood pumping
Pulses accelerating

Falling in love can be a blur...especially at **180 mph!**

So if you crave the thrill of the chase—on and off the track—you'll love

SPEED DATING
by **Nancy Warren!**

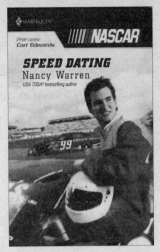

Driver coming **Carl Edwards** |||| **NASCAR**

SPEED DATING
Nancy Warren
USA TODAY bestselling author

Hearts racing
Blood pumping
Pulses accelerating

Falling in love can be
a blur…especially at
180 mph!

So if you crave the thrill
of the chase—on and off
the track—you'll love

SPEED DATING
by **Nancy Warren!**

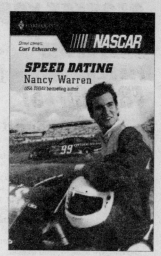

REQUEST YOUR FREE BOOKS!

2 FREE NOVELS PLUS 2 FREE GIFTS!

HARLEQUIN®

INTRIGUE®

Breathtaking Romantic Suspense

YES! Please send me 2 FREE Harlequin Intrigue® novels and my 2 FREE gifts. After receiving them, if I don't wish to receive any more books, I can return the shipping statement marked "cancel." If I don't cancel, I will receive 6 brand-new novels every month and be billed just $4.24 per book in the U.S., or $4.99 per book in Canada, plus 25¢ shipping and handling per book and applicable taxes, if any*. That's a savings of close to 15% off the cover price! I understand that accepting the 2 free books and gifts places me under no obligation to buy anything. I can always return a shipment and cancel at any time. Even if I never buy another book from Harlequin, the two free books and gifts are mine to keep forever.

182 HDN EEZ7   382 HDN EEZK

Name _____ (PLEASE PRINT)

Address _____ Apt. #

City _____ State/Prov. _____ Zip/Postal Code

Signature (if under 18, a parent or guardian must sign)

Mail to the **Harlequin Reader Service®**:
IN U.S.A.: P.O. Box 1867, Buffalo, NY 14240-1867
IN CANADA: P.O. Box 609, Fort Erie, Ontario L2A 5X3

Not valid to current Harlequin Intrigue subscribers.

Want to try two free books from another line?
Call 1-800-873-8635 or visit www.morefreebooks.com.

* Terms and prices subject to change without notice. NY residents add applicable sales tax. Canadian residents will be charged applicable provincial taxes and GST. This offer is limited to one order per household. All orders subject to approval. Credit or debit balances in a customer's account(s) may be offset by any other outstanding balance owed by or to the customer. Please allow 4 to 6 weeks for delivery.

Your Privacy: Harlequin is committed to protecting your privacy. Our Privacy Policy is available online at www.eHarlequin.com or upon request from the Reader Service. From time to time we make our lists of customers available to reputable firms who may have a product or service of interest to you. If you would prefer we not share your name and address, please check here. ☐

H107

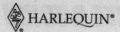

INTRIGUE®

COMING NEXT MONTH

#975 24/7 by Joanna Wayne
Bodyguards Unlimited, Denver, CO (Book 1 of 6)
The newest Harlequin Intrigue continuity, *Bodyguards Unlimited*, kicks off with a story of a first love rekindled. Jack Sanders provides around-the-clock protection, and Kelly Warner and her daughter will need every minute of it if they hope to survive the week.

#976 A NECESSARY RISK by Kathleen Long
Jessica Parker's only chance lies with Detective Zachary Thomas. But is his grim determination enough to spur her into exposing the greed spreading through the medical community—at the cost of patients' lives?

#977 JUSTICE FOR A RANGER by Rita Herron
The Silver Star of Texas (Book 3 of 3)
Texas Ranger Cole McKinney came to Justice to help his half brothers, but kindred spirit Joey Hendricks is enough to keep him there—if the secrets they uncover don't tear apart their two families first.

#978 PROTECTIVE CONFINEMENT by Cassie Miles
Safe House: Mesa Verde (Book 1 of 2)
Special Agent Dash Adams has one simple assignment: protect Cara Messinger. But the Navajo safe house's close quarters are an easy place to complicate affairs of the heart.

#979 WHO'S BEEN SLEEPING IN MY BED?
by Shawna Delacorte
Reece Covington returns to his cabin to find a woman he's never met asleep there. But as he unravels the mysterious Brandi Doyle, will he like the answers she supplies?

#980 MISS FAIRMONT AND THE GENTLEMAN INVESTIGATOR by Pat White
The Blackwell Group (Book 3 of 3)
When Grace Fairmont's trip abroad goes awry, she's lucky to have bad boy Bobby Finn looking after her. But can he protect the American girl from the one thing he's best at causing—trouble?

www.eHarlequin.com

HICNM0207